CURSE
AND
CROWN

Also by Irene Davis

Marie and the Mouse King

Sugar and Snow

Hawk and Hound

Curse and Crown

The Whitford Crew

Anyone But the Earl

Head Over Wheels

The Words and the Bees

SKOOKUM CREEK

SEATTLE

CURSE AND CROWN

IRENE DAVIS

MARIE AND THE MOUSE KING BOOK THREE

This is a work of fiction. Names, characters, places, and incidents are either the product of the author's imagination or are used fictitiously. Any resemblance to actual persons, living or dead, events, or locales is entirely coincidental.

Editing by Sarah Pesce
Book cover and interior design by Bonnie Loshbaugh

ISBN 978-1-941633-16-8 (paperback)
ISBN 978-1-941633-15-1 (e-book)

First paperback edition November 2022 by Skookum Creek Publishing

Visit the author's website at www.irenedavisbooks.com

For everyone who had to make their own happy ending.

CHAPTER ONE

I PIERCE the linen with my needle, sharp as a hawk's talon, and slide the thread through the tiny space between the warp and weft. Slowly, a wing takes shape, spreading as wide as my thumb across the cream-colored cloth, and the fabric and thread in my hands transform into something new and useful: an embroidered handkerchief.

The Aschenbrandts' parlor is full of young women, all of us holding onto the comfortable pattern of the sewing circle even as the other parts of our lives threaten to unravel. A few weeks ago, we could hear the rumble of artillery with the windows shut.

The front has moved further off from our city since then, and some of those who fled have returned, but we need the distraction of sewing for our hands and stories for our thoughts. It's too much to always be thinking about what might happen next with the war.

This morning, Florina Hatt has been telling a tale about a peasant with three sons, each of whom went out to seek his fortune in the world and met an old man who offered them gold, silver, or the chance to learn an art. When Florina finishes, Petra Aschenbrandt lays down her pen and comes to me.

"Marie, I have something for you," she says, leaning close to keep her words just between us.

I look up into her eyes, wide and blue and smudged with nights of restless sleep. I doubt my appearance is any better. The war has changed everyone in the city. We're all hollow these days. Hollow-eyed, hollow-cheeked, hollow-hearted with missing the men who've gone away and missing meals as the supplies into the city grow scarcer.

I tuck my needle safely into the half-finished handkerchief. "What is it?"

"Step out with me," Petra says.

Laying my needlework aside, I follow her from the parlor into the hall. She leads me to the drawing room. The space is wide and empty, with no party to fill it. The drapes are drawn, but the summer sun and heat seep in anyway, making the air thick and stifling. In the parlor, at least the windows were open for a bit of a breeze.

"Here," Petra says, holding out a folded sheet of paper. "This is for you. I got a letter from Ernst, and it was enclosed."

I recognize my name on the outside and my brother's handwriting. It's unsealed. "I didn't read it," Petra says as I take the letter from her.

From the gleam of curiosity in her eye, I can tell it's the truth. Still, she suspects it must be something important, or she wouldn't have called me away from the others to read it.

I open the paper and read the lines within.

Carville has given Lang over to the von Kamptz side in an exchange of prisoners. He was worth a marshal, to everyone's surprise. I know this news will hurt you, Marie, but don't waste your tears for a spy.

A spy. Given over to von Kamptz. I stare and stare at the paper, but it doesn't change its message. My brother has a very neat hand. The letters line up as orderly as soldiers on the parade ground, at complete odds with the chaos of the information they bear.

I knew Lang had lost Carville's trust, but I never suspected that Carville would give him over to von Kamptz, especially once he knew the king was Lang's uncle.

King Karl killed the rest of his sister's sons. I don't expect he will welcome his last nephew with a loving embrace.

Petra puts her hand on my arm. "Is it bad news, then?" she asks softly.

At her touch, I realize I'm shaking. My blood has run cold, even on this warm summer day. "Yes," I say. "It is bad news."

It's a death sentence for Lang. And even worse, it's not just that he'll be killed, but that he'll be killed by the very enemy he's been working to exact his revenge upon.

"Do you want to sit down?" Petra asks.

I shake my head. I don't want to sit. I want to fly straight to Lang and pull him away from danger—if it's not already too late. "When did you receive this?" I ask.

"Yesterday," she says. "I'm sorry, Marie. I thought it would be a message from your lieutenant."

No wonder she had such a sparkle in her eye before. She

thought she was giving me a love letter. "No," I say. "It's from Fritz."

I take a breath and try to settle my thoughts. Ernst must not have written of Lang's supposed betrayal to Petra, but in all likelihood, someone else in the regiment will find the news interesting enough to pass on. Fritz has made sure that the information reaches me quickly, but Petra is only the first of many who will ask me about it. There's no point in dissembling.

"My lieutenant has been traded away to the emperor's enemies," I say.

Petra's hands fly to her face and she gasps. "Oh no!" she says. "But why?"

"They think he was a spy," I say. I know he didn't betray the emperor's cause, so the words aren't too bitter in my mouth. The bitterness is in knowing that Lang wouldn't have had to expose his connection to von Kamptz if it hadn't been for me.

It's bitter, too, for Fritz to call Lang a spy. He should know that Lang wanted nothing more than for the Grand Army to bring about King Karl's downfall. I thought that Fritz saw Lang as a friend. Even after all that's happened, they were still comrades at arms. How quickly people can change their ideas about each other.

Petra has recovered a little from the shock. "Oh," she says softly. "I'm sorry, Marie. Truly, I am."

She squeezes my arm, and I let her hug me. We've never been as close as I am with Trudy, but she is a friend. As she pulls me close, I resolve that one day I will tell her my story, my whole story. There's not time today, though.

"Thank you for giving me the message," I say. "I hope you'll understand if I leave early today."

"Of course," Petra says. She hesitates, then asks, "Would you like me to fetch your things?"

I nod with relief. The thought of returning to the parlor with everyone else seems overwhelming right now. I need to concentrate on how I'm going to get to Lang.

Petra leaves me in the drawing room, and I sink down on one of the chairs.

I should never have left him—but I couldn't stay with him in the spring. I didn't know how to fly yet, and I needed the time over the summer to practice my skills.

Since the spring, I've become adept at using my wings and at traveling back and forth to the dream world. Neither skill will help me find Lang in a von Kamptz dungeon, though. I can only travel through the Kingdom of Dolls to a place that I can picture. I've never visited anywhere in King Karl's realm, and I can't hope to fly so far.

It's an impossible situation, but I've found my way through more than one impossible situation before. I unfold Fritz's note again. *Don't waste your tears for a spy.*

On a second reading, it seems less callous and more like a message within the message. My brother knows me well. He knows I won't sit around and weep, and I certainly won't weep over Lang being a spy, for I know he's not.

The letter was unsealed, even if it was hidden within Ernst's letter to Petra. Petra might not have read it, but anyone else along the way could have. Fritz wouldn't have written anything that would get him in trouble as well.

"Marie?"

I look up. Petra has returned, with my best friend Trudy at

her side.

"I'll walk home with you if you want," Trudy offers.

I nod, then take my sewing bag from Petra and tuck it under my arm.

"I'm sorry," Petra says again.

"It's not your fault," I say. "And I'd rather know, so thank you."

Trudy follows me out. We stand under the shade of the apple tree beside the Aschenbrandts' front door. "Petra told me they say Lieutenant Lang is a spy," Trudy says. "But that can't be true, can it?"

"Of course not," I say.

Sudden, swift anger rolls through me. How dare Carville trade Lang away? He should have trusted in Lang's loyalty. He would have, if I hadn't gone into the camp and raised too many unanswerable questions. But I wasn't a von Kamptz spy any more than Lang was. I don't know if I care particularly for the emperor, but as long as he seeks to crush von Kamptz, I would do anything in my power to assist him and his army.

But I'm only one woman, and even if the war has come uncomfortably close to my home, there's little I can do to influence the general, let alone von Kamptz or the emperor.

"What are you going to do?" Trudy asks. "I know you're going to do something."

"Come with me out of the city," I say. I don't know yet what I'm going to do, but I can't stay within the walls for another minute.

CHAPTER TWO

TRUDY and I walk together out the eastern gate. The guards give us the usual warnings about wandering beyond the city walls, but we all know that the front is far to the south now.

The most pressing dangers of the forest are the wild boars and bears, and the count's hunting parties have already killed most of them. If we happen to find a boar who's been crafty enough to elude the hunters, or a deserting soldier who's made it away from the army without being scooped up and returned to the front—well, we've been warned.

As we head away from the city, we pass farm women and small goat carts going the other direction. The Grand Army has requisitioned the horses and the oxen from all the surrounding countryside.

If I hadn't left my father's gelding, transformed into a wooden toy by Lang's magic, in the dream world, then he would've been taken by now. My father would've given him up gladly, but we live within the city and don't miss the horse. For the farming families who've lost their livestock, though, I don't know how they'll work the fields. A goat can pull a cart, but not a plow.

Starvation in the coming winter seems a far larger threat than bandits or wild animals in the woods, and Trudy and I aren't the only ones who've started going out into the forest to search for what might feed our families. I'm the only one who hunts with wings and talons, though, and Trudy is the only one who knows it.

She takes my hand in hers as we walk. "We're almost to the trees," she says.

Almost out of sight of the walls. Almost to where we'll turn off the path and into the forest. Almost to a place where I can change my shape without anyone seeing it. I glance up at the sky, the deep flat blue that shimmers in the heat, as if it were some brightly glazed bowl overturned above us. I want to fly up and shatter it, let hot shards rain down until there is nothing but cold night.

I need to be off the dusty ground and up in the air. I need it so badly. My heart aches with worry for Lang, and my head is thick with tangled thoughts. My bones are heavy. As soon as I can take flight, the wind will—

I stop short so suddenly that Trudy is caught off-balance by our linked hands and stumbles against me.

"Marie?" she says uncertainly.

"The wind," I say. "She promised to tell me. She *promised*." I let go of Trudy's hand and lift my skirts, hurrying into the trees. It would've been more convenient if I'd gone home to change into a pair of Fritz's old breeches, but when I have my wings, it won't matter. First, though, there's someone I need to talk to.

"Southwest!" I call unceremoniously. "Mademoiselle Southwest!"

I pause in the sun-dappled shadows, listening. I hear my breath, and Trudy's. The chatter of a squirrel tells the other forest animals of our presence. The air is heavy with the scents of pine sap and dry earth. Warm sweat slides down my spine.

"Southwest!" I yell again.

Trudy looks at me, alarm moving over her face. We're far enough away from the road that no one will see me transform into a hawk, but not so far that no one will hear me yelling for the wind and think I've taken leave of my senses. "Mariechen," she begins, but then the warm air stirs, and she goes wide-eyed and silent.

There's a thunderclap out of the clear blue sky and then the sound and the air coalesce into a young woman. She wears a loose white shift and her curling black hair is unbound. The swirl of hair doesn't hide the annoyance on her wide face, though.

"Well?" says the Southwest Wind.

"You promised to tell me if any harm came to Dietrich Lang," I say. I should curb my emotions, but Lang is in danger, and that's worth annoying the winds for. "He's been taken prisoner by his uncle, and the news has come to me by letter from my brother. Why didn't you tell me?"

She draws her dark brows together. "But no harm has come to him," she says. "There's nothing to tell."

"Have you seen him? Where is he?"

The Southwest Wind shifts on her feet. In a human, I might think the movement a nervous one, a sign that she is less than truthful, but she is a wind. She simply cannot be still. "I have seen him," she says. "He is unharmed."

"King Karl will kill him," I say. As soon as I say it, the anxious fear I've been resisting since I read my brother's note bursts open in my chest. It squeezes my heart and coils around my lungs. I can't breathe. I can't think of Lang as anything other than alive. It hurts too much, and I want to flee from the pain.

I turn away from the wind and bend my legs, looking to the sky. I will fly and fly, crisscrossing every land in this world until I find him.

"Marie! Wait!" Trudy grabs my arm before I can jump into the air.

I settle back onto the ground, but the fear still grips me. What will King Karl do to Lang? I have to get to him, but what if I can't find him until it's too late? What if it's already too late?

Trudy takes my face in her hands, forcing me to look at her. "Marie," she says. "You're panicking. I'm going to count, and you're going to breathe with me."

The world has gone black and fuzzy around the edges, but Trudy's blue eyes are bright and calm before me. "In, one," she says slowly. "Out, two."

She counts, and I breathe. My heart slows, and I can see the forest clearing around us again. The Southwest Wind is watching us, her face smooth and unreadable.

"You saw Dietrich Lang," I say to her when I feel steady enough to speak. "Where was he?"

She tilts her head to one side and purses her lips briefly. "He was with King Karl," she says. "But you already know that. Why does it upset you so?"

I take another deep breath and remind myself that she isn't human. She and her wild siblings don't seem to understand the kind of emotions that make a whirlwind inside my chest. "Because it will be the end of his story."

The Southwest Wind opens her mouth and laughs. "Oh, I don't think so," she says.

I stare at her, unable to form my reaction into words. Not polite ones, anyway.

She leans close and pats my cheek, a whisper of cool air running over my heated skin. "There is so much of his story left to tell," she says. "And yours too."

"Can you take me to him?" I ask. The winds helped me travel to the army camp before. They could do it again. But in the spring, I made a bargain with their mother and traded three stories of my life for her assistance. I don't have a new story now, and I'm not surprised that the wind is already shaking her head.

"You're not a fledgling anymore," she says. "And neither is your lover. You'll find a way to him, and later you'll come and tell Mother how you did it. But I won't take you. None of us will, so don't bother calling on any of the others."

"But do you know where he is?" I ask. "Can you describe it?"

"No," the Southwest Wind says. "I can't tell you." She smiles, her mouth just a little too wide. Her face is so close to mine that I should be able to see my reflection in her pupils, but I can't. There is only darkness at the center of her eyes.

A chill goes through my body, and I'm the one who steps back.

"When you have a tale for Mother, we can take you to her," she says. "If you don't finish it yourself, we'll tell her what we can. That is what we offer."

I swallow hard to clear the dryness in my throat. "Very well," I say. "Thank you for your information, Mademoiselle Southwest."

"We'll always be with you when you fly," she says. "And I wish you luck, Marie Stahlbaum."

She sounds friendly again, almost teasing, but I can't forget that glimpse of the nothingness in her eyes. She's not human. She may have taken a human form to speak with me, but at her core she's still an elemental force of nature.

Even as I think it, she spins away, losing shape and becoming an invisible rush of moving air again.

I turn to Trudy, who is wide-eyed. She's seen me shift my form, and she's listened to my story of meeting the winds, but this is the first time she's personally encountered one.

"She was…interesting," Trudy says. "But not particularly helpful."

"Yes," I say. I smooth my hands over my skirts. "Thank you for helping me breathe."

"It's something Father has me do," she says. "When a patient is too upset to calm themselves."

She looks around the forest again, as if the Southwest Wind might whirl back into existence. I don't expect the wind to return, but she did at least provide a little bit of information. If no harm has come to Lang yet, then I still have time to get to him. The winds believe that I'll be able to find my way to him, so I must believe it too. The alternative isn't worth considering.

My body is jittery with emotion, though. I remember the reason I was running into the forest, before I thought to call the wind. "I still need to fly," I say to Trudy. "I'll catch something so we don't return empty-handed, and then I'll figure out how I'll get to Lang."

She nods, then turns her back to me. She watched me transform once, but only once. Even for the surgeon's daughter, who's seen blood and bone since her earliest years, the sight of my body changing from one thing to another is unsettling enough that she avoids watching if she can. Still, she always offers to come with me into the woods, and we've become adept at working together on the hunt.

I can't see myself when I transform, but I can feel it. Only the changing shape of my mouth prevents me from crying out as my body shifts. My bones and skin and everything between reform, until I'm no longer a woman standing in a forest clearing.

When the transformation is complete, my first thought is to get off of the ground. I hate being so low. I can't see what is happening, and anything might trap me. I flap my wings, and Trudy turns around.

She knows my feelings and crouches to let me step onto her hand. I perch on her fist, taking care not to sink my talons into her skin. When she feels me settle, Trudy stands again, lifting me up: I spread my wings and take the momentum she gives me to launch into the sky.

Chapter Three

UP, UP, I fly, until Trudy is a half-hidden figure within the cover of the trees.

The river beyond the forest glints silver in the sun, but I don't want to go to the river. There's a meadow a little to the east of where I left Trudy, the grass burned pale gold in the late summer.

I look and almost immediately spot the movement of a rabbit. My hawk-self fixes on it. It's prey, and I'm a predator—but instead of diving at it, I circle in the sky. The warm air currents press against my breast as I mediate the internal struggle between the hawk instinct and my human mind.

It's a familiar fight, and concentrating on it does just as much to calm me as Trudy counting out my breaths. I want the rabbit, and I want to pause and plan the action of my hunt, just as I must plan my search for Lang. I've always been impulsive, but I'm working on it.

The rabbit nibbles the yellowed grass. I take care not to let my shadow cross the animal as I float in the sky above. I don't want to spook it before I'm ready to chase it, and I'm not ready yet. It's time to sort out my thoughts while I'm in the air and with a bit of distance from my problems on the ground.

I can't fly to Lang if I don't know where he is, nor can I pass through the dream world to find him, so where can I go? My brother might be able to help me, or at least be more willing to try than the winds, but I have no way to find him, either. The emperor's Grand Army is fighting on multiple fronts. His regiment has probably changed position a dozen times in the last week alone and never been in a location that I could picture and wake myself into from the dream.

The winds could carry me—but they won't, and I don't want to be beholden to them, anyway. I wish Fritz had sent me something more useful, like a map of the von Kamptz dungeons. He wouldn't have such a map, of course, but someone in the Grand Army will.

Someone like General Carville. He definitely has a map. And, oh, but I *would* like to have a word with General Carville, if I could only get to him.

I think of the general, smug behind the heavy wooden desk in his command tent like a spider in the center of its web. He's probably sitting there now. Wherever his troops have marched to, the tent and all its furnishings will have been broken down, put into a wagon, and transported with him.

I don't know where Lang or Fritz are, but I can picture the general in his tent. It doesn't matter where the front is, what duchy or principality Carville and his command have passed through, what town or village he's closest to. The general's tent will be the same—and that's the solution to the first of my problems.

I can travel through the dream to General Carville. Once

I'm there, I'll get the map from him somehow, find my bearings, and find Lang.

With that course of action settled, I feel much better. I let my attention return to the meadow and the rabbit below. It's still there, unaware of its approaching fate. First, I'll get the rabbit, then I'll get whoever hurts Lang.

I spiral back down to the clearing where Trudy has been waiting with her own thoughts. As I perch on a branch, a squirrel chatters at me and skitters up the trunk into the denser foliage. I ignore it. Perhaps the day will come when I must hunt squirrels, but not today.

Trudy looks up at me. "Are you feeling better?" she asks carefully.

I bob my head. *Yes*.

She looks relieved.

I lift my wings and hop along the branch.

"Did you find something?" she asks next. "Should I follow you?"

I nod again and lead her to the edge of the meadow where I saw the rabbit. She waits in the shade of the trees, knowing what will come next.

I climb up into the sky again. The rabbit hasn't gone far. All is still and lazy in the meadow. No soldiers march through to trample the grass. No cannons fire to send the animals scurrying. There's no hint here of the battles fought between the emperor's Grand Army and the forces of the von Kamptz king—but there will still be blood and death.

One more circle, then I glide back toward the meadow, fold my wings, and stoop from the sky.

I was careful with my shadow, but still the rabbit senses my approach and bolts. Strong hind legs kick dust and bits of dry grass into the air.

I swoop after it. My focus narrows to the flash of white tail as the rabbit flees before me. The faster it runs, the more urgent my need to catch it becomes. It dashes left, then right, then left again, but I know where the entrances to the warren are and which way it will dodge next. I take the straight path, closing the distance.

I am wings and speed—and then I am talons and tearing. The speed of my flight becomes the strength of my impact as I strike the rabbit into the dry grass. My talons puncture the soft, furry body. It screams—and then it's over.

The animal's body goes limp beneath me. I spread my wings over it, but Trudy is already hurrying across the grass. I look up and see her, red-faced and perspiring in the heat of the afternoon. There's a smear of dirt across one of her cheeks. The human form is not so well suited to moving through the forest as a hawk.

"Shall I take it?" she asks.

I haven't moved away from the rabbit. The hawk in me wants to keep it, to stay with my wings mantled over the warm corpse, and begin pulling the soft fur from it. I can't do that. Trudy and I have told everyone that Fritz showed me how to tie snares, and a snared rabbit doesn't end up missing chunks of fur. It's hard enough making sure that no one questions the punctures my talons leave.

Slowly, I fight down the hawk instincts, until I can sidle away and let Trudy collect the rabbit. She lifts it by the back legs, holding it away from her skirts. "You should take it to Luise," she says.

I bob my head in agreement. My sister is expecting her second child, and is hugely, miserably pregnant right now. Of all of us, she needs the rich food the most.

"Do you want to fly again?" Trudy asks. "I think I heard grouse calling earlier."

Grouse are a flying prey, a different challenge than a rabbit fleeing across a meadow. Today, I want a challenge, just so I can tell myself that I'm good enough, fast enough, strong enough for whatever stands between me and finding Lang. I indicate my agreement, and we begin looking for the grouse.

In the end, we have two game birds to go along with the rabbit when we emerge from the forest, tired and a bit more rumpled than respectable young women are supposed to be. Most everyone has other things to worry about these days, though, so I don't expect anyone to take notice when we return to the city.

"I'll be gone for a while," I tell Trudy before we re-enter the gate. "I'm not sure for how long, but I think I can make my way to General Carville. After that I'll find a way to Lang."

Trudy takes a deep breath and nods. "When will you leave?" she asks.

"Tonight," I say. I need to prepare a few things, and I need to find the courage this time to tell my family. If I disappear and they never know what became of me—I can still remember the anguish on my mother and sister's faces when Clara was missing. I can't do that to them again.

"I'll come visit after dinner," Trudy says. "I have some things you might take." She reaches over to catch my hand in hers and squeeze my fingers. "I know you'll find him."

"I will," I say, because there's no other option.

I send Trudy away with the grouse, over her protests. She has two younger sisters, but it's only me and my parents in our house. And since I'm leaving tonight, soon it will be only my parents.

Inside the city walls, I hurry toward my sister's house, trying to smooth over my feelings. I don't want my sister to know my worries about Lang—but if I intend to tell her this time that I'm leaving, then I'll have to explain why.

I didn't think that Fritz would ever understand the presence of magic in my life, and maybe he doesn't exactly understand it, but he *has* stood by me anyway. The least I can do is give my sister a chance to try to understand.

I go inside, leave the rabbit in the kitchen, then go upstairs to my sister's bedchamber. Shafts of golden light pierce through gaps in the curtains and relieve the dimness of the room.

My sister lies on her side in the middle of the bed, wearing only a loose shift and dozing in the afternoon heat. She opens her eyes as I come in and blinks at me.

"I brought you a rabbit," I say, glancing down to see if there are any large spatters of blood on my dress. The sight and smell of blood make her ill. Nearly everything makes her ill these days. My clothing is clean, or clean enough, and I hurry on. "I had news from Fritz today. So he hasn't been killed."

She nods. "What news?"

"Well, he didn't write anything of himself," I admit. Drawing out the paper Petra gave me, I go to sit on the bed beside Luise. "Here. Read for yourself."

Luise scans the paper and looks up at me. "Oh, Marie," she

says. "You poor darling." Before I can say anything, she wraps one arm around me and pulls me into an awkward, sideways hug.

"It's not true," I say into my sister's shoulder. Gently, I push away and sit up. "I know it was a mistake. He's not a spy. He would never help von Kamptz."

Luise looks at me. I hold her gaze, looking into familiar hazel eyes.

"We need to talk about what happened last winter when Clara disappeared," I say, and then I tell her everything.

Chapter Four

I TELL my sister all the stories: about the nutcracker and Godfather Drosselmeier on that long ago Christmas in my childhood, about visiting the Kingdom of Dolls with Lang to rescue Clara last winter, about my travel this spring, not to Nuremburg, but to the army's garrison with the help of the winds. She listens, and yet she's still shaking her head when I finish.

"Either I'm feverish," Luise says, "or you are."

"Don't say that," I tell her. "Believe me. Believe Clara." I clasp her hands in mine.

"I thought you'd grown out of this," my sister says. She glances at me, then closes her eyes and rubs her hands over them. "And Clärchen has an imagination just as big as yours."

"It's not imagination. Fritz knows it's true," I press. "And don't you remember that Christmas when Godfather brought the nutcracker?"

She shakes her head. "I don't remember much about it," she says. "Johann was courting me. I wasn't thinking about you and your toys. I remember you and Fritz fighting, but that was nothing unusual. You two were always squabbling."

She blinks, then lays back on the mattress, pressing her hand over her belly. "The baby's awake," she says. "Do you want to feel?"

Luise grabs my hand and sets it on her stomach, where her taut skin stretches her shift. We both wait. I can feel the prickle of sweat sliding down my spine and the heat of my sister's body under my palm.

Why can't she trust me? I don't know what else to do, short of transforming in front of her, and I don't want to do that. Working magic takes energy. I've changed to a hawk and back already today. It would be foolish to exhaust my reserves before I even leave home. I'll need energy to move through the dream world.

The baby shifts beneath Luise's skin. It won't be long now before my new niece or nephew is born. I want to be here to greet the baby, but not if it means losing Lang. I draw my hand away and move to the middle of the room. If I have to transform to prove magic's existence to my sister, then I will.

"Look at me, Luise," I say.

She lets out a heavy sigh, but she doesn't sit up or even turn her head toward me. Instead, still facing the canopy above the bed, she says, "I don't want to believe your story."

"It doesn't matter if you want to believe or not," I say. "That doesn't change the truth of the world."

There's a long silence. Finally, Luise says, "If there's magic in the world, what am I supposed to do? How do I keep Clara safe if magic can take her away at any moment?" She breaks off, but not before I hear the hovering tears in her voice.

Suddenly, my mother's refusal to listen to my story about the Kingdom of Dolls is cast in a whole new light. I return to the bed and thread my fingers through hers. "Godfather is gone," I say. "He's never going to steal another child. But even if there was still a threat to Clara, pretending that a danger doesn't exist isn't a protection against it."

Luise lets go of me and levers herself carefully into a sitting position. "You're all grown up now," she says softly. "And someday Clärchen will be too, and I don't know what I'll do."

"You'll protect her as well as you can," I say. "And listen to her. As long as she trusts you to hear what she's saying, she'll tell you what happens in her life."

My sister nods. "Mother didn't listen to you," she says.

"No."

"And now she doesn't know."

"No," I say, thinking of the hundred small moments of confusion and hurt when my parents wouldn't, or couldn't, listen to me telling them what had happened. I don't want that for Clara.

Luise sighs and rubs absently at her swollen belly. "I will listen," she promises. "To Clara, and to you."

"Thank you," I say.

Her gaze sharpens on me. "You're about to rush off to do something stupid and heroic, aren't you?" she asks. "You know the reason you and Fritz were always fighting was because you're too much alike."

"I have to help Lang," I say. "He helped me fetch Clara back."

"And you love him," my sister says.

My throat is tight, and I can't quite say the words back. I

nod in reply.

"Very well," Luise says. She pushes herself off the bed before I can offer to help her and crosses to the washstand. She takes a cloth, dips it in the bowl, and wipes her face and neck before she turns back to me. "You're going to go after him no matter what anyone says."

"Yes," I say. There's no point in denying it.

My sister nods. She runs the damp cloth over her arms before returning to sit on the bed next to me again.

"Tell Mother and Father that I asked you to come and stay here," she says. "To help with Clara and with the house. I hired a girl after Lotte fled, but she's gone off too. I would've thought she'd be pleased to have a place behind the city walls, but she wanted to go back to her family and I couldn't keep her. Then if Mother visits, I'll say I sent you off on an errand. I can probably keep it up for a few days."

"I'll ask Trudy to stop by and help you," I say.

"I won't be able to cover for you forever," my sister warns. "And I don't want to have to decide what story to tell Mother or Clara if you don't come back, so you'd better come back."

"I have every intention of coming back," I say.

Luise nods. "One more thing before you go," she says.

"Anything," I tell her.

"Clean the rabbit," she says. "If I have to deal with raw meat and blood, I'll be sick."

I promise to clean the rabbit and turn toward the door, but she calls me back again. "Marie," she says. "You're different now."

"I know," I say. I used to be a child, waiting for my fairy-tale prince to come for me. Now, I'm done with waiting. Lang might not be a prince, but he's mine, and I'm going after him.

Luise waves me closer, then points to the mirror on her dressing table. "Look at yourself," she directs. "Your eyes have a yellow ring around the middle."

I lean over the dressing table and peer at myself. The late afternoon sun slants directly in the window at this side of the room. My pupils have contracted to tight black holes, making it easy to see that my sister is right. There's a deep golden circle at the center of my eyes, ringing the pupil inside of the hazel brown that has been my eye color for as long as I've been aware enough to see it in a mirror.

"Hawks have golden eyes," my sister says, "and your eyes never used to look like that. So I suppose I have to believe you. I can see it plainly on your face."

I stare for a long time, but my eyes don't change. The golden circle is perhaps a quarter of the iris. Is it growing? Has it been expanding all these months, starting as an imperceptible thread of different color and only now becoming wide enough to see? Or was it an instant change the first time I became a hawk? I haven't made a habit of looking into the glass this summer, so I have no way of knowing.

When I turn around, Luise is lying down again, drawing slow circles on her belly with her fingers. Her voice is distant and thoughtful when she speaks.

"I want to say that you aren't the sister I knew, but maybe I just didn't know you." She turns her head to look at me, though the movement of her hand doesn't cease. "You're right. I'll listen to Clara when she wants to tell me. And when you come back with your lieutenant, I'll listen to your story too."

I nod. "Thank you, Luise," I say, and leave her, going down to the kitchen. I skin the rabbit and cut it up, changing it from a small animal to portions of meat in a pot. I bring wood for the stove and sweep the floor, then head back out into the street.

The afternoon is slanting toward evening now. My father will be coming home from his work, and so will Luise's husband Johan, bringing Clara back from his sister's house where she's been spending the days playing with her cousins during Luise's confinement.

Once the sun has set, the air will cool and I will slip away. I will go, quite literally, into the night, and into the dream, and when I wake, it will be to confront General Carville. I square my shoulders and head home.

Chapter Five

When I tell my mother I'm going to stay at Luise and Johann's house, she nods and tells me what a good girl I am. My stomach curdles, and my smile falters. All the things I've been brave enough for, and telling my mother all the truths of my life isn't yet one of them. I hug her, and after dinner I hug my father too before they go out to walk together as the air cools.

Dora has gone home for the day, and there's no one to ask why Trudy slips in through the garden gate so late in the evening.

"I wish I could come with you," she says as we walk up to my bedchamber. "If it was just that Lieutenant Lang was wounded, and you needed help to nurse him, then I would go with you to bring him home, but..."

She trails off, and my thoughts finish the sentence. But instead I must find Lang and bring him away from wherever King Karl has locked him up.

"I talked with Luise," I say. "I told her everything, and this time she listened. She suggested telling Mother that I'm staying with her. Can you visit and see if she needs anything tomorrow? There's no one to help her now."

"Of course," Trudy promises. I think she looks relieved to have a duty to fulfill here, but then she continues. "You can come back for me if you need to, right? You could pass back through the dream world and come to this room, or to my bed-chamber. I won't leave the city, and you'll be able to find me. If he's wounded, I could help."

I nod. It's no small thing she's offering. Trudy has been helping her father with his work more and more, and she's amassed a considerable knowledge of surgery and medicine. "There's no one I'd rather trust with an injury."

"There's always the chance that you won't be able to get him to me," Trudy says, "so I have a few things for you." She opens the reticule she's carrying and begins laying items out on my dressing table.

"This is laudanum, for pain," she says, pointing to a small brown bottle. "It should only be taken a few drops at a time. Too much will send a person to sleep."

Next to the laudanum she adds a curved needle and a skein of thread, not the colored embroidery floss we use to decorate handkerchiefs and pillows, but something thicker and undyed.

"These are for sewing wounds, but don't close a wound if it's not clean, or it'll putrefy inside and cause more harm than good."

I look at the sharp point of the needle and try to imagine stitching together flesh like cloth. All I can think of, though, is the way it felt when my hawk's talons sunk into the rabbit earlier today. "If I need to do that, I'm coming back for you," I say.

Trudy looks at me with a clear and steady gaze. "If you

can't get me, then you can do it yourself, Marie. You have dealt enough with flesh and blood."

She means the rabbits and the game birds I've killed over the last months, some with my beak and talons, some with my hands. I've lost count of how many small deaths I've caused.

I swallow and nod. "I'd still rather have you."

She looks into the bag again, takes out a scrap of blue cloth, and sits down with a more mundane needle and thread.

"If a wound isn't clean," she says, "you must make it clean. You can heat a knife in a fire and use it to burn away putrefaction. Give laudanum first, or alcohol, because people generally scream. If the wound is fresh, then you can wash it with alcohol before you stitch it. And after, you must watch and see that it has a red or yellow scab over it. If it weeps white or green, then cut it open, clean it, and try again."

She holds up the blue cloth, which she's stitched into a small pouch. "I'll put the things into here, and hope you never need to use them."

"Me too," I say.

She tucks the needle, the strong thread, and the laudanum into the pouch and holds it up, showing me where she's made two small holes in the cloth so I can thread my necklace through it.

Since there will be no one to gossip about its significance where I'm going, I take Lang's ring from the chain and slip it onto my finger instead. The golden key that was once my godfather's I leave on the necklace. I've learned that it will open any lock I set it into and I'm not leaving such a useful object behind.

The little pouch feels strange against my skin, even though

it's a smooth satin fabric. I'll have to get used to it, though. Trudy is right to send it with me. I don't know what state Lang will be in when I find him. I should be prepared for the worst. I'm going to the front of the war, after all.

"Help me cut my hair," I say.

"Really?" Trudy asks. "Must you?"

"It will grow back," I say. "I'm not going to go amongst the soldiers wearing skirts. I don't want long hair either."

I unpin my hair while she takes up the scissors from my sewing bag. It spills around my shoulders. As soon as Trudy begins snipping it away, I feel lighter. It's almost as if I am lifted up by the wind, though I don't have my wings.

"You'll have to wear a turban when you come back," Trudy says.

"Yes," I say, but I'm not thinking about that. When I run my hands through my hair, which now barely reaches my shoulders, it feels good. I twist the ends through my hands, pressing them against my fingertips, then tie it back into a queue, like a man's hair.

I wrap the coil of hair Trudy cut off into a handkerchief and push it into the back of one of my drawers. Then I stand and hug my best friend.

"It's time," I say. "Let's go outside."

We go downstairs and into the night. I breathe in the scents of the back garden, warm and green, spiced with the herbs Dora has planted to use in the kitchen. A light breeze licks around us, but it doesn't have anything to say to me.

Trudy grabs my hand, though. "Be careful," she says. "Please, Mariechen."

"I will," I promise. I give her a hug, then I take a step back and slip into the dream.

Moving into the dream world is a different feeling than changing my shape. Everything around me transforms while I remain fixed. I close my eyes against the burst of light that accompanies the transition, and the first thing I notice is the smell of the air. The atmosphere of the dream world has an indolent sweetness to it. The rose water lake is the strongest scent, but it's not the same as smelling a rose or even a whole bush of roses in the waking world.

I open my eyes. I'm standing in the bedchamber of the summerhouse. The window is open, letting in the sweet-smelling air and providing a view of heavy purple clouds tinged with the last colors of sunset. Beside me is the bed Dietrich Lang and I once shared.

I could lie down right now, sleep for just one night before I continue on to deal with all the trouble that waits for me in the waking world. A good night's sleep here, and only a few minutes will pass for everyone else. The temptation is strong enough that I'm already walking toward the bed before I catch myself.

I can't stay here. I shouldn't stay, not even for a minute. A minute could be too late for Lang.

Instead of the bed, I turn to the wardrobe. The ensign's uniform I borrowed from my brother and wore during my spring adventures is inside. Quickly, I take off my dress and change into the uniform instead. The breeches cling to my legs in ways that skirts never do, and the jacket buttons tightly over my breasts. I could probably do something to flatten my chest, but I'm not really trying to pass for a soldier. I only need to pass the first glance.

Once I've dressed, I close my eyes again and set my mind to recalling the general's tent. Wavering canvas walls, thick carpets to cover the ground, brass lamps hanging from the ceiling supports and their light falling onto the general's massive, paper-strewn desk. There was a coal brazier in the center of the tent when I first saw it, but it won't be needed in the summer's heat.

Again, the air changes. The scent of roses disappears, replaced by a hard smell of dust and gunpowder smoke, and the rusty scent of blood.

I open my eyes and find myself face-to-face with General Carville.

Chapter Six

The general's cheeks sag a little more than when I saw him in the spring, and the stubble on them is more white than gray. His mouth is open, and he blinks at me in confusion. Then he swipes a hand across his eyes and looks at me again.

I take a step back, wanting distance between us before he recovers from the shock of seeing me appear. The last time I was in this tent, I was a hawk, and the general was using threats against me to force truths out of Lang.

I wanted to interrogate Carville about Lang, and why he sent him away. Face to face with him, though, all I can think about is how it felt with the nightmarish weight of the woolen blanket wrapped around my wings. I couldn't fly. I couldn't do anything.

I can't let the general trap me again, not when I have to get to Lang. I turn and stride out of the tent before I can find out how the general is about to react.

Once I'm outside, I turn to the side, skirting around the edge of the tent in the shadows. My heart is hammering too loudly for me to think. What was my plan? *Don't let them catch me.* That's all the plan I have right now.

Through the canvas wall, I hear Carville bellow.

"Sturm!" he yells. "Bring her back here!" He's using the false name I gave him when we met in the spring, before everything went wrong.

I crouch in the dark, trying to count my breaths the way Trudy did for me.

No one has me trapped. I'm not a hawk. They don't know I could become a hawk. All I've done by walking out is make it look more like I'm the von Kamptz spy Carville must suspect me of being.

I didn't even notice if there was anyone else with the general, but he probably wasn't alone. Now there are multiple people who've seen me appear from nowhere in the general's tent, and then dart out. That was not in my plan, but obviously my planning skills still need work.

What would Lang have done if he were here? He would've stayed to talk with Carville and come up with some plausible excuse for being there. Or he would've found a place to appear that wasn't so suspicious as the middle of the damn tent. The partitioned sleeping space, for instance.

It's too late for that, though. I have to do something now. I wish I could find Fritz, but there's no guarantee that he's anywhere near the general. He could be sent away to carry messages, or scout the surrounding terrain, or requisition supplies from the villages, or a dozen other things. Connecting my brother with me would only cause him trouble, anyway.

My breathing is better now, and my heart has slowed. I should have taken a moment in the general's tent to look for the map, but there's no time. I should change to my hawk form and take to the air, where I can look down on the camp and assess where I am, and where the von Kamptz forces are.

It's too late to fly, though. "Ha!" says a voice. Someone grabs my arm and hauls me out of the shadows.

I try to pull out of his grasp, but he twists my arm behind my back so I can't turn away without pain shooting through my shoulder. Immediately, I stop struggling. If I hurt my shoulder, I'll never be able to fly away. Better to wait for a safer moment before I make an escape.

The man propels me back to the front of the tent and inside. Only then does he release me. I turn and see his face.

It's the same meddling colonel who recognized the features of the von Kamptzes in Lang. All my panic alchemizes into anger. If it weren't for this man, Lang would still be serving the general as a trusted messenger, not locked up wherever his uncle has put him.

I spit in the colonel's face. His eyes pop open, wide as a frog, in shock. Then he slaps me hard enough that my head whips to the side and my thoughts spin.

I blink and glare at him. "Touch me again," I say, "and I promise you'll regret it." When I have talons, I'll tear his face to ribbons.

"Colonel Tieck," says General Carville. "You are dismissed."

The colonel wipes his face and looks at the general, opening his mouth on some protest.

"Dismissed," the general repeats, his tone icy.

Tieck gives me a murderous look, which I return, then he salutes and steps out.

"Sit down, mademoiselle," General Carville says.

I sit in the chair he points to, telling myself that it's because I want to rest, not just because he told me to. Then I look around the tent, trying to assess my options and hoping I'll spot the magic map I gave Carville in the spring.

Colonel Tieck is gone, but there's still another man here. His head is bandaged, and the white linen wrapped about his forehead contrasts with his dark hair. He wears a plain white shirt, with no uniform jacket to hint at his rank, but Carville hasn't ordered him out. He sits in the other chair before the desk, watching me contemplatively. Though he appears younger than the general, there's a sense of authority around him that makes me sit up straighter.

Carville goes around the desk to sit in his own chair, which creaks softly. The desk is covered with the same piles of reports and dispatches and maps I remember from the spring. I can't see any sign of the magical map, but Carville's had plenty of time to find a better hiding place for it than tucked between the pages of a book.

"Mademoiselle Sturm," Carville says.

I look into the heavy disapproval of his gaze and find myself tilting my chin stubbornly. "What have you done with Lieutenant Lang?" I ask.

The man with the bandage leans forward in his chair, his interest sharpening on me. I don't know who he is, or why the general didn't order him out with Colonel Tieck, but I don't think I care.

"You wouldn't be here if you didn't know the answer to that," the general says. "The real question is why you're foolish enough to come here. You must know he's gone, so what do you wish from me?"

"Information," I say immediately.

"And what do you have to trade for it?" he asks. There's a greedy gleam in his eye as he looks at me.

"I have nothing to give you," I say. "You've already squandered what you had. You betrayed a loyal man and sold him to his enemies, and yours, when he would have served the cause of the empire to his last breath. And for what?"

"For my freedom," says the man with the bandaged head.

"Who are you?" I ask, before I remember what my brother wrote in his letter.

"Marshal Verdugo," says the man.

A marshal—I've heard Fritz speak in reverent tones of the marshals. It's a rank higher than general, reserved for those the emperor trusts to act in his name without question or consultation. They are men who know the emperor personally, the ones who served alongside him in the early days of the Revolution.

I'm already sitting, so I can't bow or curtsy, but I nod my head respectfully to him. "Forgive my rudeness, my lord."

He grimaces. "We did away with lords," he says. "Marshal is plenty, or sir. I'm a blacksmith's son, not an aristocrat."

"Sir," I repeat. "I have no doubt that the emperor and all the republic are happy for your release, but it brings me no joy to know that an innocent man was traded away for it."

Verdugo looks at Carville, who makes a sound of annoyance into his mustache.

"Lang is far from innocent," the general says. "He's King Karl's nephew. There can be no innocence there."

"On that account, sir, you are correct," I say. "The king

killed his family, severed all family bonds, and broke the innocence of Lang's earliest years beyond repair. But he's been a victim of his uncle's treachery, not a participant, and so in your eyes should be innocent."

Carville removes his glasses and rubs the bridge of his nose. When he puts them back on, he speaks not to me, but to Verdugo. "Marshal, do you recognize this young woman? Was she, perhaps, at von Kamptz's court?"

The marshal considers me. He's trying, no doubt, to imagine what I might look like in female court dress rather than a rumpled ensign's uniform. His gaze doesn't linger on my body, though. Instead, he fixes on my face. For a moment, I'm afraid he'll see everything about me. He'll turn to General Carville and announce that I am half hawk, half witch, a creature of magic that should be sent to the guillotine, or the fire, or both. Cold sweat prickles over my skin.

But all the marshal says is, "No, I don't know her."

"Where did you come from?" Carville demands. "How did you come here?"

I close my mouth and cross my arms over my chest, sitting back stubbornly in the chair.

"I sent Colonel Tieck out, and I will discipline him for striking a woman," the general says. "But I warn you now, mademoiselle, I have little patience for your games. Tell me how you came to be in my tent."

"An interesting question, indeed," says the marshal. "It seemed as if you appeared out of thin air. How did you do it?"

"First, tell me where King Karl is holding Lieutenant Lang," I say to the marshal. "Where were you kept? Can you describe it to me?"

"I had use of a little room at the top of a tower," the marshal says. "The same, I was told, that served as the princess's nursery when she was small. I rather thought princesses, even infant ones, lived in greater luxury, but perhaps they redecorated for my stay. Where Lang spends time in his uncle's company, I imagine, is more comfortable."

His description is no help, but what did I expect him to tell me? "Well, follow the river for a bit, turn left when you see a big rock, and when you get to King Karl's palace, just knock, and they'll bring your lover right out." That's not going to happen. What I need is a map. What I need is the magic map.

"Well, mademoiselle?" the marshal asks. "I have given you an answer. I await yours."

"I came through a dream," I say.

The marshal frowns at me. "A dream?"

"I don't understand exactly how it works," I say. "I can't explain more than that."

"How convenient," General Carville says acidly.

"As convenient as the map I gave you," I reply.

Something flashes across his face at my words. Guilt? Surprise? Regret? Then his expression hardens again. "Indeed," he says. "But perhaps you can try to explain further. I don't like uninvited guests suddenly appearing in the midst of things."

"There's no one else who could pass through the dream and come here," I say.

The general hasn't taken his eyes off me. I was hoping that he'd glance to some particular direction and give me a clue where the map is hidden. If there was a corner sticking out from a book, I'm sure I'd spot it.

The mention of the map hasn't escaped the marshal's notice, though.

"What map?" Verdugo asks.

"A map as wondrous as my appearance in this tent," I say. "A map I gave to General Carville on our last face-to-face meeting."

"Is that so?" the marshal says. "Bring it out, Carville. I'd like to see such a thing."

Carville grits his teeth and glares at me, but he leans down behind the desk to unlock some drawer or compartment I cannot see. There is the rustle of papers, then he brings out the folded sheet. He stands, but he doesn't hold it out to the marshal.

If the marshal sees the map, it will be a confirmation that Carville has met with me before. Whatever conclusions he draws from that will be General Carville's problem, not mine. My problem is how to get the map, and then how to make use of it.

"Well," says the marshal. "Give it here."

Carville shoots me another resentful look and holds out the map.

Before the marshal can make a move, I force my tired body out of the chair. At the same time my fingers snatch at the map, I wish myself to the dream world, yawning so hard that my ears pop and my eyes close involuntarily.

The blood and gunpowder smell of the army tent is again replaced by rose water. I open my eyes—and shriek in horror at the sight of General Carville standing before me.

CHAPTER SEVEN

THE general is just as surprised as I am. He lets go of the map, so I take the opportunity to step away from him and tuck it into the waistband of my breeches at the small of my back. My arms and legs tremble with weariness.

I need to lie down, but the general is peering into the purple darkness of the night around us. Maybe I shouldn't worry so much about my inability to plan ahead. It doesn't seem like anything ever goes to plan, even when I have one. My plans never included General Carville standing with me on the shore of the rose water lake.

"Take me back," Carville says. "At once."

"I would like nothing more," I say. "But I can't."

I've already transformed myself twice today and moved between worlds three times on top of that. Six transformations sent Lang into a state of utter exhaustion. If I hadn't been there to pull him out of the snow, it would have killed him.

Working any magic right now would leave me unable to stand, let alone defend myself. Returning to the army camp would be the height of stupidity.

"Unacceptable," Carville sputters. "I don't have time for your games, Sturm."

"Yes, so you've said," I say. I look past him, to where I can see the glow of lights from my summerhouse. It occurs to me that I could send him away as I did with Godfather Drosselmeier when he confronted me in the nutcracker's castle.

A few yawns, and Carville could wake—but where? Unfortunately, I can't guarantee that he'll return to his command tent. It was a mistake that brought him here, but I don't want it to be a mistake that turns the tide of the war in King Karl's favor.

"You can't keep me here," the general says. He strides toward me, and I step back on trembling legs.

He should have let go of the map. I should have tugged it out of his grasp in the tent, but I was too focused on making my escape before he could trap me. Now I've trapped Carville, even though I don't want him.

"I'll return you in the morning," I promise. "Time moves differently here. You'll only lose a few minutes in the waking world."

He lifts his hands, as if to grab me by the shoulders and give me a good shake, then stops. His hands drop, and he harrumphs angrily. "Why are you doing this?" he asks.

"For Lang," I say, returning his anger with my own. "You sent him away, and now I have to find him."

I can't see his expression in the dark, but I can guess that the general is glaring at me. "I curse the day you and he met," Carville says.

"And I the day he met you," I return.

I'm sure that I knew Lang first, even if it was before I knew he was a man. I'm equally certain that I know parts of Lang that the general can't even begin to suspect, but it strikes me that Carville must know Lang in an ordinary, everyday way that I don't. Lang served as the general's aide for months. They worked side by side, shared meals, had a thousand of those small interactions that build up a relationship between two people.

I could hate Carville just for that.

"Be grateful that I'm willing to take you back at all," I tell the general. "If the Grand Army didn't need you, I might just leave you here."

It's a waste of breath to stand around arguing with him. I turn away and walk toward the summerhouse. It's not far, but right now I feel like it will take me all night to get there and I can't let the general see how weak I am.

"Where are you going?" Carville demands.

I wave ahead, where the lights seep through the trees. "There's a house."

"Whose house?" he asks suspiciously.

"Mine," I say. It's difficult to be polite when he's not trying either, so I ignore him and continue walking. One foot in front of the other. It shouldn't be so hard. Once I get to the summerhouse, I can lie down and sleep.

"What is this place?" the general asks. He's following me, of course. "Is this your dream, Sturm?"

"Yes," I say. "This is my dream." It's not mine alone, but that's a detail the general doesn't need to know. He doesn't need to know anything about the nutcracker or the Kingdom of Dolls. He just needs to wait until I have the wherewithal to take him back to the waking world.

Carville stops asking questions, though I can hear him grumbling under his breath behind me. I concentrate on following the path.

We draw close to the summerhouse, and the gravel drive crunches beneath our feet. The windows are lit by lamps, showing the red shutters beside them. The summer night here is mild without oppressive warmth. It would all be perfectly wonderful if I hadn't accidentally dragged General Carville here with me.

Even if I don't like him, however, I can acknowledge he didn't ask to be here. My experiences with magic haven't always been entirely pleasant, but at least I've had the privilege of choice every time I've come to the dream world.

Carville is still muttering. Finally, he bursts out with "What is that scent?"

"The lake is filled with rose water," I tell him. "It's quite lovely in the sunshine."

"Rose water?" he says, disbelief and disapproval clear in his tone.

"It's *my* dream," I say. "Perhaps I like the scent."

I did like the scent, once. Now I hardly notice it. I reach the door that enters into the first floor of the summerhouse, push it open, and turn back to the general.

He stands at the edge of the light spilling from the house, hesitating. Of course he would be too suspicious to simply walk into a strange place.

I don't have the patience for dillydallying, though. I have the map. Everything else can wait until morning, when I don't feel as if I'm going to fall over at any moment. I need to sleep so I can return to my search for Lang.

"Stay outside if you wish," I say to Carville. "But there are beds inside, and food, and comfortable places to sit."

He glowers at me, and I see he has a pistol in his hand. I should've guessed that he'd have a weapon. Here I am, trying to be at least somewhat hospitable, and he's thinking that I'm leading him into a trap. The whole dream world is a trap, but he doesn't know that. He hasn't met the nutcracker and seen what happens if you stay here too long. He hasn't felt the pull to simply remain in the dream and forget all the horrors of the waking world.

I step through the door before he gets any ideas of holding me hostage against whatever enemy he imagines waits inside the house. "You can sleep outside," I say. "It will be warm enough. There are no large animals."

"You keep no servants?" he asks.

"There's no need for servants," I say. "Everything is provided for." I point at his pistol. "And that won't work here." At least, it won't work now that I've seen it and taken the time to think about what would replace black powder in the Kingdom of Dolls. He won't have much luck igniting poppy seed paste, and he's going to have to clean the entire gun once he realizes it.

Carville leaves the pistol pointed at the ground, but he doesn't step into the summerhouse. I shrug, trying to look nonchalant rather than exhausted, and go up the stairs. They are stone, the same as the walls of the ground floor. When I reach the first floor, the construction changes to wood, with soft, thick rugs covering the planks of the floor.

I glance toward the windows that look out over the lake, as I do each time I come here. The image of Lang standing there, so deep in thought that he doesn't see the view, is imprinted so strongly in my memories that I always half expect to find him here. I never do, but I look just the same.

I wonder where he is in this moment. I hope he's still safe—or safe enough. He has to be, since the Southwest Wind hasn't come to tell me otherwise. Traveling into the dream is no difficulty for the winds. She could find me if she wanted to.

General Carville comes up the stairs behind me and steps into the open room. He, too, looks to the windows and the lake. "What is that?" he asks. "A city?"

"Yes," I say. Lights cluster on the far shore of the lake, illuminating the outlines of the nutcracker's city, the capital of the Kingdom of Dolls. I still haven't been able to bring myself to return there since Lang and I found my niece Clara where the nutcracker had taken her away to hide in the towers of his marzipan castle. Maybe after I find Lang, I'll go and look, just to see if there is some sign of the nutcracker's fate.

For now, though, I wave at the table, which is covered with dishes. "There is food. Help yourself. You'll find a bedchamber upstairs if you wish to sleep."

The general nods slowly. I leave him staring at the unfamiliar view as I climb the stairs to the second floor, enter the bedchamber, and finally, finally, reach the bed. I pull off my boots and lie down, not bothering with any other undressing. Something crinkles uncomfortably at my back, and I remember the map. I take it out of my waistband and set it on the bedside table.

Since I'm already in bed and about to pass out with exhaustion, I use a bit more of my energy to remove the door to the room, leaving a smooth white wall both inside and out. Now the general may wander the house as he pleases, but he won't be able to find me, or the map, until I'm awake and ready to face him. Once that's done, I close my eyes and slip away into a dreamless sleep.

Chapter Eight

I HALF wake and roll over, intending to go right back to the dream where Lang and I were flying together. The motion brings the painful stabbing sensation of pins and needles in my arm, though. The dream evaporates, and I'm in the whitewashed bedchamber of the summerhouse. It's fully light—I've slept until midday.

I lie still, sorting through my thoughts and shifting my arm in slow increments until the blood is flowing through it again and I can use it to push myself to a sitting position.

I feel much better than I did last night. I'm awake and alert, and I want to take to the wing and fly and hunt. I want a nice big rabbit in my talons—I stop the thought and laugh softly at myself as I stand and stretch. I'm ravenously hungry, but I won't be flying this morning. There's far too much to do before I can fly again.

In the mirror, my reflection is strange. My hair falls loose around my face. It takes a moment to remember that Trudy helped me cut it. Trudy will be waking in her own home now—

no, it will still be evening for her. Trudy will be going to bed and wondering if anyone will ask her where I've gone. The marshal with his bandaged head will still be in the general's tent, wondering what I've done with Carville. And Carville? I listen, but no sound reaches me through the walls of the summerhouse.

How has he spent the hours while I've been sleeping? I have no idea, but now that I'm awake, there's no sense in putting things off. I pull my hair back and tie it with the leather cord that lies on the dressing table the moment I wish I had one. It's a small thing, and I only realize I wished it into existence after the fact.

I need to be careful with my wishings, though, and save my energy for my next steps. First, I must bring the general back to his tent, and then I must escape from him and the Grand Army in order to make my way instead to where the von Kamptz forces and Lang are.

For that, I need the map. It's on the bedside table where I left it. I sit cross-legged on the bed and spread it over my lap.

At first, it appears to be an ordinary map, heavily marked with colored flags. The standards were more scattered last time I saw it, with the different armies mostly still in their winter garrisons. Now they clump together near the names I've learned as battlefields in the newspapers. The emperor's standard is perilously close to the capital of von Kamptz's kingdom, so where is von Kamptz?

I trace the lines of the map with my finger, the rivers and mountains and so many different tiny flags. They aren't moving now, perhaps because it's night in the waking world. My finger drifts across the markers, and one placed between a river and the von Kamptz capital catches my eyes.

It's not red or green or pink like the other flags. Instead, it shows a pattern of interlocking rings. My heart skitters at the sight of it. Even before I count the rings with a trembling finger, I know how many there will be: seven. I count again. Seven rings, seven crowns, seven circlets for Lang's seven murdered brothers.

On my hand, the ring Lang gave me flashes suddenly in the light. I take it off and turn it in my fingers. There's a dark smudge covering part of the metal's shine.

I rub at the spot, then scrape with my fingernail, but it doesn't come off. The ring has never tarnished before. Even when I had all seven of them, I never once had to clean them. They always shone and sparkled.

Fresh unease curls in my belly. Did the wind lie to me? Or has something happened to Lang that the winds can't see? I imagine him in a dungeon, somewhere so deep beneath the earth that no breath of moving air can reach him.

No.

No.

Lang is unharmed. Southwest will tell me if anything hurts him. I don't yet know how or why his uncle is keeping him alive, but I will find him. There is no other option.

I fold up the map and slide it carefully into an inside pocket of my attila jacket. Then I pull my boots on and bring the door of the room back into being.

When I step out onto the landing, the summerhouse is quiet. Is the general asleep, or waiting somewhere below? He could've gone outside to take the morning air. He could've grown tired of waiting for me to reappear and set out to walk to the capital.

That last thought sends me quickly down the stairs. It's bad enough that I brought the general here. I don't want him wandering around the Kingdom of Dolls at will.

As I reach the bottom of the stairs, however, he's sitting on the divan with his boots off and his feet propped up. There's a bookshelf that was definitely not part of the furnishings before, and Carville is reading a book bound in dark green leather.

I already suspected that the dream world might respond to the wishes of whoever found themselves here, but that bookshelf is a confirmation. Now I really have to get the general out of here as quickly as possible, before he realizes he can influence this place.

"I find your library unexpectedly well stocked," Carville says, looking up.

"Is that so?" I say warily.

He nods, holding his place in the book with one finger. It looks to be the essays of Montaigne.

"I don't often find myself with the leisure to read," the general says.

Is that a hint of wistfulness I detect in his voice? He seems oddly relaxed, considering the state of irritation I left him in the night before. I'd be a fool if I didn't take advantage of this mood of his somehow.

"Then I'm glad to have given you some small leisure," I say.

I surprise myself with the words, for I actually mean them. Despite everything he's done, there's a part of me which wants to like General Carville. The first time I saw him as a hawk, I wanted to tear at him with my claws, but when I'm human I can see that he's not a wicked man. He has his goals, and since they are those of the emperor and the Grand Army, it's inevitable that they don't always align with what I'm seeking.

My brother respects this man, I'm sure. Lang must have too, or he would've left long before the general betrayed him. That knowledge holds me back from my more instinctual animal dislike of the general, especially when he's sitting here with a book and looking so entirely benign. I still can't trust him, though.

"You've given me time to think, and much to think on," Carville adds. He follows me to the dining table.

I've slept, but I still need to eat. I'm itching to leave, to fly, to act, but it's not quite yet time. As long as I'm in the dream world, there is time enough for breakfast.

"How did you come to pass into dreams?" the general asks. "You told me a tale of a brother in the emperor's army, but now—I wonder. Are you Lang's dream, or is he yours? Where did you begin, Mademoiselle Sturm?"

I don't like these questions. The less he knows, the better. I've already given him too much time, as he says, to think and too many things to think on. "I began in the waking world, as did you," I say. "And it is coming time for you to return."

At the table, there is fresh bread and butter, and wheels of cheese alongside bowls of ripe fruit. I sit down and begin putting food on my plate.

"What are the boundaries of this dream?" the general asks. He waves his hand toward the window and the view across the lake. "What is there in the city that lies across the water?"

"It is much the same as any city," I say, and turn away to my food.

He sits down at the table, still watching me. The seat he's

chosen is the chair where Lang sat when he was here. When he was with me. The thought twists hard and painful inside me. I'm no longer hungry, but I eat anyway, because I know I must. I need my strength. I can't have my body collapse when I have so much to do.

When I've eaten all I can stand to, I push back from the table. The general, too, comes to his feet. I reach across the table and lay my hand on his arm. "Time to wake," I say.

Chapter Nine

Carville blinks at me, then he yawns. We slip between worlds, and I hold the image of the army tent tight in my mind: lamps, carpets, the marshal sitting in the chair before the desk.

When I open my eyes, we're back in the evening we left a day ago, or perhaps only a few minutes ago. The marshal starts up from the chair, his eyes widening.

General Carville whirls around, far faster than I thought possible for a man of his age, and clamps his hand around my wrist. "How long has it been?" he asks the marshal immediately. "How long have I been gone?"

"Not more than a quarter of an hour," Verdugo replies.

I tug at my hand, but the general's grip is strong. I can't slip back into the dream world without taking him with me again. I can't shift into hawk form either, or I will easily be trapped within these canvas walls.

"But how? What happened? Where have you been?" the marshal asks.

"In Mademoiselle Sturm's dream, apparently," Carville says.

"A quarter of an hour, you think? And perhaps fifteen hours passed in that place. This could change everything, Verdugo. If we could give the men a night's rest in ten minutes—and that is only the beginning." He moves to his desk, tugging me along with him. "You may keep the map, mademoiselle, if you will assist us in this. The emperor will owe you a great debt."

He wants me to bring soldiers into the dream world? I shake my head. "No. I can't do that."

"Can't?" he asks. "Or won't?"

"I can't," I say firmly. "It's not possible to take more than one or two people with me at a time." As soon as the words are out, I wonder if I should've played at ignorance instead. I wish I'd lied to Carville when I brought him with me. I should've made him think that I'd never transported anyone else into or out of my dream before. "I shouldn't even have been able to bring you."

He shakes his head. "But you did it once. You can do it again."

"Not for an entire army," I say. "It can't be done."

He glares at me. His hand on my wrist is painful enough that I concentrate on holding very still. If he lets go, I'll return to the dream world, and he knows it. If I'm patient, though, there will inevitably be a moment when his attention slips.

"What are you talking about, Carville?" asks Marshal Verdugo.

"She took me with her into the dream, as she said," the general replies. "By accident, but what a happy accident! It's a land by a lake, with a comfortable house. Everything was peaceful and still as a country estate before the Revolution. I would've stayed a fortnight if I wasn't needed here."

He pauses, and adds, a little wistfully, "Perhaps I *could* stay a fortnight."

The marshal snorts. "Listen to yourself, Carville," he says. "What soldier is going to return to the battlefield from such a place?"

Carville opens his mouth, closes it again, and frowns.

I think I understand a little how he feels. The dream world changes with your expectations. It can be very seductive when you expect it to be a pleasant place. Even with no knowledge of what his thoughts might do, General Carville found a bookcase in my summerhouse because he expected to find such a thing there.

"It can be much harder to leave the dream world than to enter it," I say. "Even if I could bring your soldiers there, I wouldn't do it." What the varying ideas of a company's worth of soldiers might do, I shudder to contemplate.

"What am I to do with you, then?" Carville asks. "I don't know what you know, Sturm, but I know it's too much for me to let you roam free."

"I would still like to see the map you were speaking of before," Marshal Verdugo says.

"I left it in the dream world," I lie immediately. "For safe-keeping."

"It's my map," Carville growls. "You gave it to me. We had a deal."

"You did little enough to hold up your end," I reply. "So I'm taking the map back."

"Carville," Verdugo snaps, in a tone of voice which ought to remind the general that he isn't the highest-ranking officer in the tent. "What was on this map?"

"Everything," Carville replies. "It's enchanted. It shows the whole theater of the war, and all the most current locations of every fighting force."

The marshal's eyebrows rise. "Truly?"

Carville nods. He hasn't let go of me yet, and he tugs my wrist as he points at me with his free hand. "She brought it to me in the spring. It has—it *was* very useful."

"And you," the marshal says with dangerous calm, "kept it for yourself."

"Yes," Carville says slowly. "I did, but—"

"Imagine what a boon such a map could have been to our emperor," Verdugo says. "Imagine how he might have used it for planning and directing his campaigns these last months."

It's very satisfying to watch the blood drain from the general's face. It would be more satisfying still if the shock caused him to release me, but apparently I'm not to be so lucky.

"Imagine how many lives might have been spared," the marshal continues. "The resources that might have been used more efficiently. The battles that could have been won *if the emperor had that information.*"

"I didn't know if I could trust it," Carville protests. "I didn't know if anyone would believe it if I showed it to them."

"You are too narrow in your thinking," the marshal replies, "and you assume everyone thinks the way you do."

He stands and paces the short distance between the desk and the closed entrance of the tent. "You think the emperor doesn't know of the existence of magic? All information flows to him, and he knows things you can never dream of. You think you could send soldiers from the battlefield to another realm to recover for the next campaign? If such a thing could be done, the emperor would know. We would be doing it already, as would von Kamptz."

What response the general might make to this, I don't know, for the flap of the tent is pushed aside and a young ensign of the hussars bursts in.

The ensign goggles at me, and at the general holding me. His mouth actually falls open. He's quite young, younger even than Fritz was when he badgered Father into letting him finally enlist. No hint of a beard mars his chin, though he's smudged with dirt.

"Report, ensign," the marshal says.

The ensign closes his mouth and stands up straight. "Yes, sir," he says. "I went to scout along the enemy's camp, as General Carville assigned me. I saw"—he pauses, looks nervously back and forth between the marshal and the general—"I saw Lieutenant Lang with them, sir. With a uniform all in gold braid. I didn't believe he was a prince, but he must be, after all."

I listen as the ensign answers questions from Verdugo and Carville, describing the movement of the von Kamptz troops and Lang's position among the enemy's marshals.

Who is this ensign? Carville calls him Keller, but it doesn't matter what his name is. He must be mistaken. Whoever he saw, it couldn't have been Lang. Lang would never lead his uncle's troops. He would never side with the uncle who had the rest of his family killed. He told me as much, and I heard him swear it to General Carville too.

The general, though, doesn't seem surprised. I have ample opportunity to watch his face, since he keeps me held beside him. No, there is no surprise there. It looks more like smugness, as if things are going according to his plan.

How can he not be shocked by this news? Perhaps it is some plan of his. But what plan? I cast my mind back, trying to remember each detail of that terrible conversation when the general forced the confession of Lang's lineage out of him. Lang swore he would see King Karl fall, that he would see him dead.

The general laughed at that last, saying that von Kamptz would be exiled rather than assassinated, but that was before all this summer's long bloody campaigns. What if he changed his mind, and decided to put Lang in place to assassinate the king?

My blood runs cold at the thought, for if Lang succeeds, what will happen next? I know firsthand that it is not so simple to fly away when an escape is required, and Lang can't slip into the dream world the way that I can. Even if he can make the transformation to hawk or mouse and flee from the guards who must surround the king, General Carville doesn't know that, or he would have figured out by now that I am one and the same with Lang's hawk.

The ensign has finished his report, and there is a sudden silence in the general's tent.

"You sent him to die," I say.

"He volunteered to go," Carville replies.

Chapter Ten

"Ensign Keller," the general says. "Come and hold onto this young woman."

The ensign looks at his commanding officer, then at me. "Sir?" he says uncertainly.

"She can't escape if someone is holding onto her," Carville says. "Not without taking you with her."

This statement doesn't make the ensign look less confused, but he comes forward and reaches hesitantly for me.

"Hold her tightly," Carville says. He passes me to the ensign, who wraps cold fingers around my wrist and blushes. I make no move to protest or struggle, but my heart leaps. No matter what the general commands, I know I have a better chance of escaping from the ensign's hold than Carville's. The months of flying have built up strong, wiry muscles in my arms. I'm stronger than I look, and the young ensign won't expect me to be.

"Take her out of here," the marshal says.

"No," Carville says.

The ensign looks between the two officers. He's probably been used to following every order of Carville's—but the marshal outranks Carville. Poor boy. I can feel the tremble of indecision in his hand on mine.

"I won't go back to the dream world," I say. "Nor would I take your ensign with me, General. You have my word."

Carville looks at me with narrowed eyes, obviously ready to object again.

"Try to keep her if you must," the marshal says. "But she can't be here listening to our every conversation. I am satisfied that, whatever she is, she is no spy. But there's no need for her to learn any more than she already knows."

The general harrumphs, but he swallows his objection. I follow the ensign into the night, still trying to play meek.

Once we're outside, the ensign relaxes a little. "What am I supposed to do with you?" he asks. "And how long am I supposed to hold on to you?" He sighs and looks off to the left.

I can't tell in the dark what might be in the direction he's looking. But since he presumably came directly to the general with the report from his scouting trip, I think I can guess. "You must be hungry," I say. "And now that you're stuck with me, you can't even get a bite to eat."

"I had field rations," he says. His eyes stray away again, but he recovers himself and tightens his grip on my wrist. "What did Marshal Verdugo mean?" he asks. "When he said 'whatever you are.' What are you?"

He suspects something. Or maybe this question is somehow important to him, because he asked it with an intensity I didn't expect. It's a personal question from Keller, not the ensign following the general's orders.

What am I? Am I a woman, or a hawk, or something from a dream? I am a fairy tale, like the ones Petra writes down. I'll be collected someday, and bound between leather covers alongside women who went into the woods and came back with pearls falling from their lips or with armfuls of nettles to weave into fine cloth.

"Never mind," the ensign says into the silence I've left. "Forget I asked."

But the ensign isn't asking what magic I've seen. He's only trying to figure out what my place in this war is, why I was in the general's tent, how long my presence will keep him from food and sleep. The general is right to think that I won't make the same mistake twice. I won't take this youth into the Kingdom of Dolls. I've promised not to, and I won't break my word—but I never promised not to do other magic.

I roll the idea around in my mind as I stand in the sleeping army camp, hand in awkward hand with the unhappy ensign. The marshal wasn't surprised to hear of magic maps or the dream realm. He was the emperor's envoy to the von Kamptz court, after all, before King Karl broke the treaty and restarted the hostilities with the emperor.

The royal court is where all these stories start: the curse on Lang's mother and her children, the cursed princess, the cursed nutcracker. The court where Godfather Drosselmeier was once the royal clockmaker. The court where the royal astrologer cast curses, and his books taught Lang the way to break them. Anyone who spends time in that court might think, as the marshal seems to, that keeping magic secret is a foolish, antiquated notion.

If I time things right, then it won't matter if the ensign, and thus the general, learn that I'm also a hawk. I wish I could see the moment when Carville realizes Lang kept me right under his nose, but if I stay for that, I won't be able to get away.

"Where did you ride to scout today?" I ask. "Which direction are von Kamptz's forces?"

Ensign Keller blinks and points with his free hand. "West," he says. Then he pulls back and peers at me in the torchlight. "Why?"

"You want to know what I am?" I ask him. "I'm not just a woman in a man's uniform." He flinches away from my words, or from the tone of my voice. "I am Dietrich Lang's lover," I say.

"But Lieutenant Lang is—" The ensign pauses, unsure how to categorize Lang, or maybe caught on what his next words might imply about me. If Lang is a traitor, then how can I not be a spy, even if the marshal has said I'm not?

"What Lang is isn't for you to know," I say. "Just know that I'm going to find him, no matter what. Do you have a sweetheart waiting for you?"

Again the ensign recoils, as if my words are a slap across his face. He's young, but perhaps not too young to have fallen in love. Maybe I can bring him around to see my position.

"Think of the woman you left behind," I say. "If she knew you'd been traded away to your enemies—"

"Shut up!" Keller cries. "The woman I left behind is dead."

"Oh," I say. My thoughts fly to Luise, to Trudy, to Petra, to all the others waiting at home for Fritz, for Ernst, for all the men who have gone away to war. Then I realize that, in his agitation, Keller has finally forgotten the general's orders and let go of me. I take a step back and raise my open hands placatingly. "I'm sorry. I didn't mean to bring up bad memories."

He glares at me, breathing quickly, but already struggling to reassert control over his emotions.

I take another step back. I'd hoped to somehow win the ensign over to my side, to make him see that letting me go was the right thing. His reaction is entirely unexpected. Another day, I might sit down with him, ask what happened, and try to soothe the wound I've so obviously prodded—but right now I don't have time to delve into this stranger's past.

Two more steps. I'm edging toward the side of the general's tent and the pile of crates I found there earlier. Then Keller blinks, recollecting himself and his orders. "Wait," he says.

I dive away, starting my transformation in the same instant.

Magic twists my body, spinning flesh into feathers. I hit the crates, sending them tumbling. By the time everything settles, I've changed from woman to hawk.

I hop up to the top of the pile. The torches at the entrance of the tent give just enough light to show Ensign Keller gaping at me.

It's too late to say anything to him, and I don't know what I'd say. *Sorry for upsetting you? Sorry for the trouble you're about to be in? Give my best wishes to General Carville?*

I spread my wings and take off into the night.

The moon rides high in the sky. It's nearly full and it should be the brightest thing in the darkness, but the army camp below me eclipses it easily. How many thousands of men is this?

I can't count the fires spread like brilliant constellations across the land below me, and I have no frame of reference.

In the spring, I only rode through the camp and never had the chance to see it all at once as I do now. It's immense, and somewhere down there, in one of the small white tents lined up beside the fires, is my brother.

I had wanted to find him, but if he doesn't know what I intend, then he can't worry about me. On the other hand, he sent me the letter, so he must expect that I will do something. He's probably worrying already. I can't fly to him, though. He's one soldier among thousands in this camp, and even if he's here right now, I'll never find him.

I look to the moon instead, judge the direction, and bank to the west as the sound of General Carville's angry shouting begins once again below me.

Chapter Eleven

I SPEND the night in the crown of a tree, with my head tucked beneath my wing and the soft rustle of leaves singing through my dreams. A squirrel wakes me with its angry chattering in the pale glimmer before dawn. When I spread my wings, it runs down the branch, then pauses to chide me again. Ignoring it, I launch myself into the air and head away from the rising sun.

An hour's flight carries me over fields churned by wagons carrying heavy artillery, above blackened timbers which used to be towns. I circle high above the site of a massive battle. Men and horses lay strewn about like spilled grain. Flocks of carrion-seekers, some with wings and some with hands, pick them over for anything of value.

I'm glad for the remove that flight gives me. I can see the way the corpses have bloated, but I can't smell them. I fly on as quickly as I can, trying not to look at the expressions on the eyeless faces below. Lang isn't there, for Keller saw him only yesterday. I refuse to let myself think of my brother lying among the fallen, either. He was alive and writing me letters not so long ago, after all.

Beyond the battlefield is a wide, winding river, and there, spread along both banks and bulwarked around a stone bridge, I find the other army. It looks much like the camp I left earlier this morning: row upon row of small canvas tents with campfires in between them, wagons and horses interspersed. Heavy cannons are spaced around the perimeter on the eastern bank, ready to defend the river crossing against the inevitable approach of the emperor's forces.

In contrast to the varied colors of the emperor's Grand Army, though, these soldiers are mainly dressed in white. Many have red cuffs, some have red or blue breeches.

I circle closer, looking for the tent that holds the commanders. Will the king himself be here, or will his marshals be leading this defense? The emperor is known for leading his men personally—he rose through the ranks of the army before he became an emperor, after all—but the newspapers that report so much about the movements and victories of the Grand Army have had little to say about the other side's commanders.

On the western side of the river, set back from the bank, I finally find a group of officers and important-looking people clustered together. It's a good thing that I'm already gliding, for in the moment that I see Lang, I would've forgotten to flap my wings.

He stands in the center of the group, just as Keller reported. I want to go to him immediately, to pull him away with me to the dream world, wrap myself around him, and never allow us to be separated again.

But when I went running to him in the spring, everything went so horribly wrong. I must be more cautious this time. I must wait. General Carville claimed Lang went willingly to von Kamptz. I can't discount the possibility that the general was telling the truth. Being here might be part of Lang's plans, and if I take him away, I'll ruin everything again.

So I don't fly to him. I float above the river and study him. Instead of the hussar's uniform in green with yellow braid, he's dressed in a white jacket and red breeches, with a red-and-white sash across his breast. His high, stiff collar is decorated with gilt braid. There is gold, too, along the fastening of his jacket, at his wrists, and the wide sash at his waist.

I see no sign of any wound on him: no bandage such as Marshal Verdugo had on his head, no crutch to hold him up. He stands tall and straight, occasionally nodding his head at something the other officers say, or putting in a few words of his own.

The Southwest Wind spoke truly: he's unharmed. I'll owe the wind an apology once I figure out what's going on. How is it that Lang is in his uncle's power and still alive?

I glide above the men, looking at the others who stand with Lang. Only one of them has as much gold on his uniform as Lang, and when I look at his face I know he must be King Karl. Seeing them side by side, the family resemblance which Colonel Tieck recognized is immediately apparent. It's there in the aquiline nose, the slant of the eyebrow, the narrowing of the eyes as they give some idea particular attention.

Lang says something. King Karl nods and claps a hand to his nephew's shoulder, the same rough masculine approval I've seen dozens of times among my brother and his companions.

Despite the warmth of the sun on my wings, the wind suddenly feels cold. How can Lang be standing here so calmly next to the man he hates? The man who gave the orders to kill Lang's family?

For that matter, how has it come about that King Karl has welcomed his long-lost nephew into the court? Why is Lang here, reviewing maps and troop movements, rather than in a dungeon or an unmarked grave?

All this must be according to Lang's plans, I tell myself again. Perhaps he's pretending that he doesn't know or remember what King Karl did to the rest of his family. Perhaps King Karl regrets his actions all those long years ago and is happy to reunite with his nephew.

Perhaps perhaps perhaps. There are too many maybes and not enough information. I hate not knowing, but what can I do? Transform back to a woman, walk up, and ask?

No one would be pleased to see me here at the center of their command, particularly when I wear the green and gold-braided uniform of a hussar regiment in the emperor's Grand Army. I'd be shot on sight even before they realized I'm a woman.

With General Carville, I could at least trust in his honor as a gentleman and an officer. He sent Tieck away for striking me, and while he might imprison me until he can discover my secrets, I don't believe he'd harm me. Among the von Kamptz officers, however, I have no trust or loyalty with anyone but Lang, and I don't know what he intends.

I have to go to Lang, though. I can still fly to him as a hawk. I won't let anyone lay a hand on me. I won't try to take him into the dream world. I'll just let him know that I'm here, that I'm ready to help him if he needs me. He'll give me some sign, and then I'll know what to do next.

I swoop down toward the group of officers and cry out, *kek-kek-kek*.

The men look up. A few duck or raise their arms, as if to cover their faces against my talons, but I only want to see what Lang's reaction will be. He turns with the others and lifts his hand, not to protect his face but to shield his eyes from the morning sun at my back.

I bank and circle, coming back where he'll be able to see me without the light in his eyes. He blinks at me, his brows crinkled with an expression of confusion and the worry any man might feel with a predatory bird flying toward their face.

Kek-kek-kek, I cry again. He must recognize me, surely. He must. He could explain me away to von Kamptz as he did to Carville. His hawk, temporarily lost but loyal to her master.

But he doesn't lift his hand for me to perch on. He takes a step back, glancing to the other officers who are doing the same. One man even puts his hand to the hilt of his sword, as if he might slash me out of the sky.

I beat my wings, climbing out of striking range. Lang turns his head to follow my flight, his hand still shading his eyes. His bare hand, I realize. Entirely bare: no gloves in the summer heat, and no rings on his fingers.

Where are the other six circlets that he took back from me on Christmas Eve? I have the seventh and it will be on my finger when I transform again, but where are the others? They are the remembrance of his dead brothers, and I can't imagine him giving them up, not for anything.

I spiral upward, my mind twisting in confusion. I know Lang is a master at masking his emotions, but I can't escape the cold feeling that his reaction was no act. I'm glad I'm a hawk in this moment, or else I would be sick.

He didn't know me. He should have recognized me, but he didn't.

I float in the sky, catching the currents rising from the warming earth below me and trying to sort out my next move. Even if Lang hasn't been physically harmed, von Kamptz has changed him somehow. I'll have to figure out how to undo it.

A wind slips beneath my wings. I want to ask what it knows, but the Southwest Wind already told me they won't be sharing any answers with me this time.

After a quarter of an hour, I spiral down and take up a perch in a tall cottonwood beside the river. The water moves slowly this late in the summer, and I can see fish basking in the shallow pools. A soldier comes to fill a bucket, and his splashing sends the fish into hiding in the shadows of the larger rocks.

I look across the camp and find Lang's form. He's still beside his uncle, who pats him on the arm again.

Maybe Lang was only acting as if he didn't know me. Concealing his true thoughts from King Karl will be a thousand times more important than hiding himself within the Grand Army. The consequences are certainly much more dire.

I watch as Lang moves around the camp. The meeting of the commanders is over and the soldiers receive orders: suddenly everyone is in motion. The cavalry mount their horses. The infantry shoulder their rifles. They begin heading east toward the early morning sun.

Lang rides at the head of the column. As it departs, however, I see that it's not the entire force. A third of the men remain, clustered tightly around the bridge they hold. King Karl is with them, still at the command tent.

If—when—the advancing force finds the emperor's Grand Army, Lang will be the first in battle while the king will be protected. It doesn't look like King Karl has any more hesitation about sending Lang to his death than General Carville.

Carville said Lang volunteered to be traded with Verdugo. Verdugo, who was in the von Kamptz court before the treaty was broken. Verdugo, who was not surprised at magic. Verdugo, who chastised Carville for not giving up the magical map. The map that I have.

Will the marshal have some warning that von Kamptz is marching to meet his forces? I don't remember if Ensign Keller said anything about von Kamptz making ready to move. I was too wrapped up in my shock and dismay at the ensign's report about Lang to listen to the other details.

But Lang isn't the only one I have to worry about. There's also my brother, wherever he is, and the other men from our city who serve under General Carville. Without the map, the general will have to rely on scouts to report the movement of the von Kamptz forces, but what if there aren't any scouts nearby?

I can't leave the Grand Army in ignorance of the troops approaching them. I fly ahead of the column, looking for the places where a scout like Keller might be watching, but see no one. Even if there were scouts who've already turned back, what was an hour's flight for me to cross between the camps will be a longer journey for a man on horseback. I have no need to go up and down hills or cross streams. I will never stumble on uneven ground.

I look back to the men heading east. Lang is still there at the front, all white and gold and red. It hurts to leave when I've only just found him, but he's not in danger until the two armies meet, and that won't happen for hours yet. I have time to return.

One last look at his face, so familiar in its features but so unfamiliar in its stiffness, then I fly east with all the speed I can muster.

CHAPTER TWELVE

I CROSS the field of fallen men. Not until I sight the tents of the Grand Army ahead do I see a rider below. A hussar on a white horse, heading west. He's directly below me, bringing his horse up from a gully.

His face is hidden at this angle, but his uniform colors and his bearing are familiar. Ensign Keller, sent out again to gather information about what von Kamptz is doing. He should have gotten up earlier if he wanted to see what I've seen.

There's no reason not to tell him, though. He can take the knowledge to Carville and Verdugo, and I won't need to go into the camp and risk my own capture.

As he comes out of the gully, I spiral down to land in a nearby tree at his eye level. He reins in his horse and eyes me suspiciously.

I look back at him, turning my head to the left and right. There's not even the beginning of a mustache darkening his lip. The other soldiers probably tease him for being a child, but the wariness on his face says he's seen plenty of life.

Whatever else he's encountered, he's already seen me transform once. I flutter down from the tree, but I don't put myself too close to him. I still don't want to end up in a situation where I have to pull him into the dream world with me, so I make sure that the trunk of the tree is between us before I return to my human body.

"Are you a witch?" he asks when I step out in front of him. His voice is calm, but his horse tosses its head, communicating its rider's discomfort. "You must be a witch."

"Perhaps I am," I say. I know only two magics: the trick of transformation he has just seen, and the way to come and go into the dream world. The ensign doesn't need to know that, though, and a little fear of my powers on his part might be a healthy protection for me. "I have information for you to give to General Carville and the lord marshal."

Keller tightens his grip on the reins and his horse takes a step backwards. The gully is at his back, however, and the animal's instinct of self-preservation won't let him retreat further. Unless he wants to ride over me, he's trapped. "I thought you were going to seek Lieutenant Lang," he says.

"I found him," I reply. "Thank you for the direction. It's as you said, he rides among the von Kamptz commanders. But they are on the move. They're marching here."

Keller shakes his head. "But I saw them yesterday. They were fortifying the river crossing."

"Then they must have finished the fortification," I say. "I'm no judge of such things. But two-thirds of the men at the river camp are headed this way." With Lang leading them—my heart stutters. "Only a small force remains at the bridge," I add quickly. "If the emperor's men can maneuver around the column coming this way, they could go directly to the river before von Kamptz realizes they're coming. King Karl is with the forces at the river."

I don't know if the Grand Army can make such a maneuver or if Marshal Verdugo and General Carville will accept the idea, considering that it comes from me. There's the chance, too, that von Kamptz scouts will see the change in their enemy's location and bring the news to turn their own column back or to the side. I have to try, though. For my brother's sake, I don't want the Grand Army to be caught unawares. For Lang's sake, I don't want them to clash with the von Kamptz forces coming this way. I hope that King Karl and the river crossing will be the more tempting target.

Keller is still staring at me. "Why should I believe you?" he asks. "Why should General Carville take your word, when you've said your loyalty lies with Lang, and Lang is with von Kamptz?"

I wish I were a hawk. It would be far more comfortable if I were perched on a tree branch looking down, rather than standing on the ground and looking up at the mounted ensign. "I don't want him killed," I say. "If the fighting is somewhere behind him while he is marching toward opponents who have already moved, then he'll be safe." At least in this action. At least today. Tomorrow will be another question.

"Then perhaps you want to send the emperor's Grand Army on a wild goose chase," Keller says." Or simply into confusion, so we'll be that much easier for your lover to defeat."

He doesn't believe me. My heart sinks. He'll go around me and continue toward the approaching force. By the time he finds them, sees the truth of my words, and brings the report back to his commanders, hours will have passed and the chance for the

Grand Army to slip around to the bridge will be gone.

Maybe I should tell him about Fritz. Would he believe I want the emperor's victory because my brother wants it? We have been speaking German together. Keller's accent is not so different from mine; he'll know that men from my city have volunteered to the emperor's army. But he'll know, too, that there are volunteers who left to fight with von Kamptz. Both armies give a salary, after all, and not everyone cares for the emperor's revolutionary ideals.

I discard the idea. Better not to bring my brother into the discussion. Keller will report everything back to Carville, and I don't want the general to reopen the search for my brother among his men. I don't think Fritz can be traded away to von Kamptz as Lang was, but I'm sure the general could do other terrible things to him.

I shift from foot to foot, wishing again that I was off the ground. I need the perspective of height to see clearly. The motion makes something crinkle in the breast pocket of my attila, where the pelisse hanging from my shoulder drags over it. I still have the map. It will show the troop movements I've described, and the general, at least, will trust it more than he or Keller or Verdugo will trust my words. I've already found Lang, so I don't need it anymore.

I look up at the ensign. "I have a map," I say. "If you take it to the general, he will know the truth of what I'm telling you."

"I'm not going back to the general," he says. He gestures forward, over my head. "I have orders."

"This is more important," I say.

I take the map from my pocket and unfold it. My eye finds the symbol of interlocking circles at the fore of a group of red-

and-white flags moving east from the river. On the western side, beyond the crossing that von Kamptz guards, is von Kamptz's capital. No wonder King Karl is there among the defenders: the emperor is making the final approach to capture the heart of his kingdom.

"Here." I step cautiously toward the white horse and hand the map up to Keller. "Watch the map for a minute. You can see the troops moving from the river."

He glares at me, then at the paper. When he sees the map's markers shifting beneath his gaze, though, his eyes go wide. Tentatively, he places a finger on the map. I've done the same: there is nothing to feel, only the usual texture of pressed paper. Then he looks at me, and I can see from the set of his face that he's made a decision.

"You changed from woman to hawk," he says. "And back again."

"Yes," I say. This isn't what I expected him to bring up, but I can't deny him the evidence of his own eyes. I spent too many years being disbelieved about my experiences with magic; I refuse to pass that uncomfortable confusion on to anyone else.

He folds the map and taps it with his fingers. His lashes slant downward for a moment before he speaks again. "What other transformations can you make?" he asks. "Can you change another?"

I think of his accusation about my being a witch, and about the stories we tell at the sewing circle. "You mean, will I turn you into a frog if you don't do my bidding?"

"No," he says. His horse steps in place and tosses its head. Keller wraps the reins around hands gone pale and bloodless beneath the brown of many months in the sun. "Not a frog."

He pauses again, pats the neck of his horse, and then the words tumble out, low and quick. "Can you change a woman's body to a man's?"

The ensign's beardless cheeks. His recoil when I said I was a woman in a man's uniform. The fierce, anguished way he said the woman he'd left behind was dead.

I thought he spoke of a lover, but now the pieces fall into place: it was himself he meant. I think of Lang, born a mouse after his mother was cursed, and how he had to work to find the magic that would transform him into his true form.

"Are you cursed?" I ask the ensign before I can think of more tactful words.

He laughs bitterly. "For as long as I can remember. From the moment of my birth."

I look at the ensign, considering what to say next. I've given him the map, and in return he's told me something of himself. "I can't change you," I admit. Keller's mouth thins, and I add hastily, "But perhaps Lang could. He knows far more of such things than I do." I don't know all the magics Lang learned from the astrologer's books.

"Would he do such a thing?" the ensign asks.

"I think he would," I say. If anyone will intimately understand the ensign's curse of not having the body he was meant for, it will be Lang. "I'll do everything I can to convince him."

Keller looks at me for a long moment, assessing. "If you will help me, I will take your message to the general," he says finally.

"I will help you," I promise.

Chapter Thirteen

The ensign turns back toward the Grand Army with the map in his sabretache. I sit down in the dry grass and watch him go, already second-guessing myself. What if Carville doesn't take my plan? What if Verdugo doesn't believe the map and overrules him for a more direct action?

I twist the ring around my finger, then pull it off and look at the black smudge hiding the shine of the metal. Has it grown? Is Lang in more danger than before I started interfering?

The wind shifts. The sweet smell of the grass is suddenly overtaken by the terrible stench of death from the battlefield that lies between here and the river fortification. My stomach turns, but there's nothing in it for me to bring up when I retch.

I'm tempted to flee back into the dream world, where there are no armies marching towards battle. Perhaps Carville had the right of it, and I should try to take soldiers into the Kingdom of Dolls. If I could take one of the armies off the map altogether—but then what?

I'd probably kill myself in the effort, and the remaining

troops would overrun what the missing men had been meant to defend. It wouldn't end the conflict until there was no one left for either army to recruit or conscript.

If the Grand Army goes around Lang, pushes through King Karl's bridge, and takes his capital, then he will have to sue for peace with the emperor. The fighting will be over. Lang and Fritz and Ernst and all the other soldiers will return to their families, or start new families. Lang will help Keller break his curse, and the ensign will grow a mustache like every other cavalryman. When all that is accomplished, Lang and I will be able to go wherever we choose, without the guilt of things left unfinished pulling us back.

I put the ring back on my finger, stand, and walk back to the tree I stepped behind to transform out of the ensign's sight. The trunk is wide enough that I can't clasp my arms around it. It must be old. What has it seen? How many people have passed beneath its limbs, or taken shelter here from sun and rain? Next to the life of a tree, my troubles are small and fleeting—but that makes them no less pressing to me.

A tree must stand and take what comes to it, but I must go and see what I can do to affect my fate. I rest my forehead briefly against the rough bark, then step back and return to my hawk body. As soon as the change is complete, I move up into the branches and look around for animal movement. Whatever the future holds, I must eat and keep up my strength.

The gully has a small stream trickling through it, and it's not long before I spy a squirrel that has left the safety of the trees for a drink. I wish it were a rabbit, but I don't have the luxury to wait for different prey right now. Apparently, today is the day when I hunt squirrels.

I eat, and when my belly is full, I fight against the inevitable urge to drowse in the tree. Lang and the column of soldiers he leads will catch up to me eventually—or not. I no longer have the map to tell me where he or the von Kamptz forces are. By now, Lang could have taken wing himself and left his uncle's soldiers, heading somewhere I'll never discover.

The anxiety of my spiraling thoughts sends me into the air. How long did I spend trying to convince the ensign to carry my message? I look to the angle of the sun to reassure myself. It's still morning. There's still time. I wing westward, not stopping until I find the red-and-white standards. Lang is riding at the head of the column, just as I left him. The tight twist around my heart eases.

Now that he's safely in my view, I perch in a tall tree and watch. The infantry marches. The cavalry and the officers ride, Lang among them. Their pace isn't fast, but it is steady. They're not turning from the path they started out on. By mid-morning, they'll reach the battlefield of fallen men, and by early afternoon, they'll be at the Grand Army's position, if the Grand Army doesn't move.

I watch Lang until he passes below me, then I fly ahead to another tree and watch him again.

Eventually, it occurs to me that his body is oddly quiet. His mount carries him forward, but he doesn't move in the saddle. He doesn't shift his seat or readjust his grip on his reins. He doesn't look left or right at his surroundings, or down at his hands. His gaze is straight forward between the ears of his horse, but even the horse looks around at its fellows occasionally.

If I were in my human body, a chill would be sliding down

my spine. First, the rings missing from his fingers. Now, this unnatural stillness. Something is wrong here. Something is very wrong.

This isn't Lang waiting for the right moment to carry out his revenge against his uncle. This isn't Lang collecting intelligence about the enemy that he will take back to General Carville, to Marshal Verdugo and the emperor. This is barely Lang at all.

His shape hasn't been transformed this time, but some new curse has been laid on him. He should never have gone to King Karl, or to the von Kamptz court, where so many curses have begun.

First on Lang's mother and her children, then on the princess, and lastly on young Drosselmeier. Only Lang, young Drosselmeier, and the princess have survived their curses, but will they ever truly be free of them?

I think of the princess, King Karl's daughter and Lang's cousin, and the only one of the three I haven't yet met. Godfather Drosselmeier called her Pirlipat, but that was either a nickname or pure nonsense for his story, because I know she's called Paula Maria.

Suddenly, she's not just a member of another land's royal family. She's more than just a character in a story my godfather told me as a child. She's a living, breathing woman, probably ensconced in a palace in the city on the other side of the river her father defends.

Did Lang meet with her when he arrived at von Kamptz's court? Did he call her by her given name? Did he think of faraway "Marie" when "Paula Maria" crossed his lips?

I can't bear to think about it. I fly ahead again to keep pace with Lang and the other officers at the forefront. They're coming to the battlefield where the two forces have obviously met so disastrously before. Von Kamptz must have held the day that time, however, or the Grand Army would already be across the river.

The men become increasingly grim-faced as they skirt the edge of the field. Now that I'm closer to the ground rather than flying high above the corpses, the smell is appallingly strong. Some of the men retch, even among the officers, and I'm glad that my hawk body doesn't have the same reaction.

Lang remains stoic. When this battle happened, which side was he fighting with? I look to the officers who ride beside him. From the sidelong glances they give him, I think he must have been with the Grand Army, not with these men.

I fly close, circling over the head of the column, over Lang's head. One of the officers looks up, but Lang doesn't. To be so close to him and still be separated, to not even have him acknowledge my presence—it's unbearable. I fold my wings and stoop down toward him.

Kek-kek-kek, I cry. *Look up. You must look up and see me.*

Both of the men flanking Lang look up. The soldiers behind him look up. And then, finally, at the last moment, Lang looks.

I shriek again, putting all my frustrations into the piercing sound, even as I backbeat my wings to avoid crashing into him. To its credit, the gray stallion he rides, though it isn't Kuno, is well trained enough that it doesn't shy away from me or try to throw its rider.

Lang blinks at me, and a tiny line of confusion appears between his brows. Another blink. The furrow on his forehead deepens, then his gaze seems to sharpen on me. His mouth opens.

Whatever he might say, though, is swept away by the bright, brassy call of a horn. The drums begin a quick, fierce rattle that rolls down the line as one company after another picks up the beat. The soldiers begin to yell and shout. I spiral up again, and there, spread out along the eastern end of the battlefield, is the Grand Army.

Chapter Fourteen

My first instinct is to dive toward Lang. I'll take him out of here. I'll pull him into the dream world where he can't be hurt. But he's already charging forward with saber drawn and the gray stallion leaping easily over the furrowed ground. The rest of the von Kamptz force is yelling and joining in the charge, and the drums and trumpets have become a deafening cacophony. I can't concentrate my thoughts with all the noise.

At the other end of the field, the Grand Army begins its own charge. Is Carville there? Verdugo? My brother? Ensign Keller must have failed to bring my message, or failed to convince his commanders to accept it. They shouldn't be here. They should be marching to take the river crossing.

My frustration quickly turns to anger. I fly across the field to the Grand Army side, searching for the commanders. It's not long before I spot Verdugo leading the charge. His head is still bandaged, giving him a rakish air as he waves his saber from the back of a black stallion. I stoop and scream, as I did with Lang—but for Verdugo I don't try to break the dive at the last minute. I fly at his face with my talons outstretched.

He swears and ducks. Instead of tearing his flesh, I catch the bicorn from his head. I carry the hat away, drop it among the men behind him, and return to fly at the marshal again. He swings his saber at me this time, and I have to turn in the air to avoid being sliced in two. I shriek at him and fly upward, out of the saber's range.

The line of the emperor's soldiers has continued forward without the marshal, although those closest beside him paused when he did. Now their charge toward the enemy is uneven and the other side is fast approaching.

Marshal Verdugo rallies and shouts. Another soldier echoes him, and trumpets ring out again. The Grand Army continues forward, and the marshal, bare-headed, moves to regain his place leading the charge.

I wheel in the air and come from behind to sink my talons into Verdugo's right shoulder, gripping hard enough to puncture the wool of his uniform and the flesh beneath it.

He cries out, then reaches across with his left hand, trying to grab me without dropping the saber he holds in his right.

I scream into his ear and flex my talons as if I were eviscerating a rabbit. I want to tear into him with my beak as well. I could so easily remove his ear. But no—I catch the predatory turn of my thoughts and temper them. I don't want to disfigure the marshal. I just want to dissuade him from this charge toward Lang.

Instead of biting him, I beat my wings against his head and scream again. For his part, the marshal continues to yell and scrabble at me. Finally, I release my grip and push away into the air. Fabric tears as I go. Verdugo continues cursing.

This time, though, the discipline of the army has held. The Grand Army is still moving toward the von Kamptz troops—toward Lang. I can't stop all of them. There are thousands of men, and I am only one hawk.

I haven't even stopped the marshal. Blood is soaking through his jacket at his right shoulder, but he switches his saber to his left hand and wraps the reins around his right. I suppose you wouldn't end up a marshal if you'd let a little flesh wound stop you.

I wheel above the Grand Army's line again, looking for Carville. Even Ensign Keller will do. Why didn't they listen to me and go around to the poorly guarded bridge?

I can't find the general or the ensign. I look for Fritz among the mounted hussars sweeping along at the edges, but I can't find anyone in his regiment's colors. Where is my brother?

I climb into the sky, taking stock of the two forces now clashing on the field. The emperor's men are spread in a line just ahead of the trees on the eastern side, but although they present a wide front, it's not deep. The other side, which had been a long column, is gradually moving into position to meet them, but there are still more of the king's men hurrying to the field to engage.

There were more men in the Grand Army's camp, so why are they now outnumbered? Where is my brother's regiment? Where are the rest of the emperor's men?

Belatedly, I realize the marshal has done the same as King Karl: split his men and sent them to different places.

I climb higher, scanning the horizon. There—to the north of this battle is a shimmering haze of dust in the midday sun. It must be Carville, leading the bulk of the men around to the river crossing. Is Fritz there? I feel the tug to fly off and see, but I don't dare leave while Lang is in the middle of the fighting here.

I dive again, seeking the white-and-gold uniform Lang wears. He's near the center of the field, with three of the mounted von Kamptz officers beside him. A group of light cavalry from the Grand Army, with high, fur-covered hats on their heads and bright brass armor covering their chests, rushes towards them with lances.

Lang swings his saber in defense. He knocks one lance aside, and the power of his blow unseats its wielder. Meanwhile, Lang's gray stallion strikes out with its hooves, slashing at the oncoming horses.

The carabiniers retreat slightly, regroup in a tight formation without the fallen man, and rush forward again.

I swoop toward the lead carabinier. He has one hand on the reins and the other steadying the long, deadly lance, and nothing free to protect his face. As with the marshal, I strike hard against his hat. His head snaps back, but the hat doesn't come off.

Instead, I have the heart-rending realization that it has a chin-strap and I'm trapped with my talons deep in the bear skin. I flap my wings wildly, trying to release myself while the man curses. I can see nothing now but the dark fur, but he must have shifted his hold on either the lance or the reins, for he undoes the strap himself and flings the hat away.

I go with it, still flopping with my talons in the tangle of fur. My opponent didn't have the presence of mind to think about where he threw me. Together with the hat, I strike the shoulder of the next man and tumble into the space before his saddle.

He also swears at me—if I remember these words, I'll have a very interesting vocabulary when I return to my human form.

Like the first man, though, his hands are taken up with controlling his lance and his mount. There's nothing he can do to get rid of me.

I manage to get free of the horrible hat on my own and launch into the air again. It's all I can do to fly straight, but the breeze freshens beneath my battered wings, carrying me to the edge of the battlefield.

I land clumsily in a tree and take stock. Everything happened in the blink of an eye, but I must have struck the second man on my back, for that's where I hurt most. At least I landed against his arm, rather than his armored chest.

My heart skitters wildly around my feathered breast. I could so easily have broken my wings, or fallen down into the deadly forest of horses' legs and crushing hooves. No one would notice my trampled body among the fallen on this field. Perhaps one of the scavengers would pluck a few of my feathers to put in a hat, but I would get no burial and my family and friends would get no word of how I had fallen.

Of course, the magic might also return me to my human form in death. There would be some macabre satisfaction in that, for then my uniform would be recognized for Fritz's regiment and, when my body was examined, some rumor would reach my brother. It would be gruesome, but better that than my family never knowing what had happened to me.

But I'm not dead. I'm alive, though my back and one of my shoulders ache fiercely. If it weren't for the subtle interference of the wind, I might not have made it to this tree.

I want to flee to the dream world and the quiet calm of the summerhouse. I can't leave without knowing what happens with Lang, though. Has my near death done anything to protect him?

I search the field, trying to see through the clouds of smoke from the cannon fire. Finally, I see that he is still upright on the gray horse. The group of carabiniers has been reduced to only four men: even numbers with Lang and the officers beside him. The emperor's men have lost their lances. They draw their own sabers, and the two groups come together for close combat.

When the first man swings his blade at Lang, I reflexively spread my wings—and cringe at the pain that immediately radiates through my body. However much I want to protect him, I can't fly to him now.

Lang blocks the strike with his own saber, though. In the exchange that follows, I rest easier in the knowledge that he can still defend himself, no matter what enchantment has dimmed his other reactions.

He dispatches his opponent and turns to engage one of the other carabiniers, drawing the man away from the von Kamptz officers. Before he finishes this second man, though, a new sound ripples through the horns and drums of the Grand Army. The carabinier makes a last, vicious thrust in Lang's direction, then wheels his horse and gallops away.

All across the field the emperor's men are doing the same: breaking off from their fights with von Kamptz's forces and retreating toward the woods.

Lang and his officers pause, catching their breath and shouting to one another. Then they surge forward, and the von Kamptz army gives chase.

Chapter Fifteen

THE white-coated soldiers of the von Kamptz army stop short of following the emperor's men into the forest. They don't need to: they've routed the enemy. Now they gather in their squadrons to collect the fallen and tend to the wounded. The supply wagons that made up the end of the column have caught up to the battlefield, and tents are being set up.

Lang rides across the field, and I see the soldiers watching him. Their looks are respectful as he approaches, but far more wary once he's passed.

Soldiers gossip like market women, and I wonder what tales they tell about him. What story did King Karl put about to explain this sudden nephew, whom he's dressed as a prince? Do they know that, until a short time ago, he fought against them as the emperor's man?

Then there are the things that Verdugo said about magic. That the emperor knows of magic, that it is used openly, or openly enough, in the von Kamptz court. Do these men know that Lang wields magic, or that he's under some magical control?

They must have seen my flight across the battlefield, my attack against the marshal and against Lang's opponents.

Belatedly, I realize that I'll be part of the stories told by the soldiers of both armies after this battle, for better or for worse.

I try to stretch my wings again, but my body is already stiffening. One of my shoulders barely moves. It's my right side: the same one I injured last winter when Lang and I were first traveling in the Kingdom of Dolls. I remember the gruff efficiency with which Lang put the dislocated joint back in place. Even then, he was taking care of me. Now it's my turn to look after him, but there's little I can do in this moment.

Lang reaches the tents. He dismounts and hands his reins to an orderly before going behind a canvas wall where I can't see him. After my experiences at the command tent of the Grand Army, I'm wary of following him inside. The fighting is done for now. Lang will be safe, or something like it, for a little while. The best thing I can do now is make sure I'm ready to follow him when he moves again.

I close my eyes and concentrate my thoughts on the summerhouse, with the front room drenched in sunlight and the rose water lake sparkling outside the windows.

The perch beneath my talons changes. I open my eyes to the dream world, where I'm settled on the back of the sofa. I hop awkwardly down into the cushions and return to my human form.

When that is done, my shoulder feels better. It seems that the magic, in reshaping my body, is content to put it back together with all the joints and muscles the way they ought to be. My back is still painful. If I could see it, I'm sure it must already be purple with developing bruises.

There's no point in trying to contort my beat-up body to undress or take a look at my back, though. Instead, I bury my face into an embroidered pillow that smells of lavender and rose, and fall asleep.

When I wake, it's late afternoon, and my muscles are stiff as new leather. I'm almost surprised that nothing creaks out loud as I work myself into a sitting position.

I'm sweaty from sleeping in the sun, and what I want most is a bath. It feels like a wasteful luxury, compared to the position of the men who must remain in the stinking dust of the battlefield. But it's not just a luxury—it will help my sore body loosen up again.

I walk slowly through the summerhouse, imagining the bath I'll find. There's a door beyond the kitchen, and when I open it, it reveals a cozy bathing chamber full of sweet-smelling steam.

A copper tub waits in the center, half full, and there are two cans of hot and cold water standing at the ready beside it. I undress and work my way down into the water. It's a much bigger tub than my family has, and the water is the perfect temperature. Even a princess couldn't ask for more, though a princess probably has a bevy of maids to flutter around, bringing soap and towels and helping wash her hair.

With all that has happened since I left home, I'd forgotten about my hair. I have to lean my head back to wet it, and the damp ends only just brush my bare shoulders. The warm water works its everyday magic on my muscles until I feel as limber as usual. I work up a lather from the soap ball and wash my hair, along with everything else, feeling pleased at how quickly it goes now that my hair no longer reaches down my back.

When I finish the bath, there are fresh undergarments piled

on the chair where I hung the ensign's uniform that was once my brother's. The uniform itself is a little dusty, but since I've mostly been wearing feathers, it has no blood or grime from the battlefield.

As I dress, I think of the argument between Carville and Verdugo after I accidentally brought the general here. I understand both sides. Having this pleasant retreat will enable me to return to the battlefield, ready to continue with what I must do, but, at the same time, if I didn't have the drive to help Lang, I might never leave the dream world.

A hot bath no one has to carry water for, a comfortable house that never needs cleaning, food that appears with no need for chopping, simmering, salting, and watching, on dishes that never need washing… Who would want to leave such luxury behind? But I know it's a dream, and once I've dressed and eaten, I make myself a hawk and slip through to the waking world again.

I return to the tree where I had been perched, looking over the battlefield. Everything looks much the same as when I left: von Kamptz's men holding the field and busy with the unpleasant tasks that come after a battle. The scavengers who follow the armies are picking over the bodies for rings, buttons, teeth—anything that might be quickly extracted and pocketed.

I hesitate for a moment, then fly across to the place where I last saw Lang. A tall pole supports the von Kamptz banner, flying above the tent. It's just big enough for me to perch at the top. As soon as I land, the soldiers closest stare and point at me.

"Is that the hawk?" they ask one another. "The prince's familiar?"

"He sent it to attack the emperor's marshal," someone

replies.

"He used it to frighten the enemy away."

When I turn my head, trying to pinpoint who is speaking, several of the men cross themselves or make other signs against evil.

If this is what they're saying here, then what rumors are spreading in the Grand Army? Ensign Keller will know it's me, and if he told everything to his commanders, then General Carville and the wounded marshal will also know that I'm not a mindless tool of Lang's. I can only imagine the stories being told among the rank and file who will hear small threads of story and embroider them into something larger.

If Lang had any thought that he would return to his position as a lieutenant to the emperor's Grand Army, that notion must be discarded now. Once again, I've acted without thinking of the consequences, and here they are.

I fold my wings tightly, trying to make myself as small and inconsequential as a sparrow, but the soldiers still watch and murmur. How terrible it is for all these strangers to recognize my connection to Lang, when he himself does not recognize me!

As these unpleasant thoughts wrap around me, Lang emerges from the tent. A soldier follows close behind him and points up at me.

Lang clasps his hands behind his back and looks up at the standard where I perch. His lips purse thoughtfully. There is a newly livid red line on his left cheek, a shallow shadow to the slice he gave to the nutcracker in their duel last winter. One of the carabiniers must have gotten through his defenses, but there is much, much worse that he could have suffered.

He studies me for a moment more, then, slowly, deliberately, holds up his left hand. It's an invitation for me to fly to him, but there's still no light of recognition in his eyes. I hesitate, thinking of tent walls and traps and dangers that I can't yet anticipate.

But this is Lang, and I want so badly to be at his side. How can I refuse? I unfold my wings and glide down to him.

Chapter Sixteen

Lang holds himself utterly still as I settle on his outstretched hand. It's the wary caution one uses for approaching a wild animal, and another confirmation that he doesn't recognize me. I have no jesses, no bell or tether trailing from my ankles to say that I've been manned and tamed, but what other hawk would fly so fearlessly to him? If Lang remembered anything of what passed in the last year, then he would know me.

But the curious, breathless way he regards me sends doubt crawling along my nerves. Perhaps I'm the one who is mistaken, and this isn't Lang after all. It might be some other member of the von Kamptz family who shares his features. Lang might still be in a dungeon somewhere, or worse.

I tilt my head to one side and then the other, studying this man as he studies me in turn. His dark eyes are fringed by long lashes. His mustache is well shaped over his full lips. His jaw is barely shadowed with the day's beard. Apparently princes can find time for a shave before riding into battle, but since he's been made the figurehead at the front of the army, it makes sense that he must be well-groomed.

His clean-shaven cheeks, however, mean that there's no hiding the thin white scar on his left cheekbone, now with his new wound drawing a parallel line beside it. I can't look beneath his uniform for the other, more prominent scars he carries, but this line on his face is one I know. This is Dietrich Lang, and no other.

He raises his left hand and slowly, slowly reaches towards me. He touches my back, a light, tentative stroke along my feathers. When I don't lift my wings or move my head, he tries again with more confidence.

"Well, milady of the skies," he says, "who dispatched you here to me?"

There's no answer that I can make, so I only look at him.

"Whoever it was," he murmurs, "I owe them a debt of thanks for sending an avenging angel."

He strokes me one more time, then lifts his hand as if to send me back into the sky. I take the momentum he gives me and return to my perch with the von Kamptz standard.

Once again I'm glad for the remove from my human emotions that the hawk form affords me. If I were a woman right now, I'd be weeping inconsolably. The hawk's instinct, though, is to remain as close to my mate as possible, hoping that the next time he looks at me, I'll see the light of recognition in his eyes.

Lang returns to the tent and whatever business he has leading this portion of the von Kamptz army. I don't like losing sight of him, but I can't go into the tent. As long as Lang is within, I'll wait here.

The sun moves toward the horizon. Officers and aides and

messengers come and go. Though the uniforms are different, it's all much the same as what I saw when I was at General Carville's tent.

A late day breeze rises, lazily tweaking the von Kamptz standard. I wait for the wind to tell me something, to give me some clue about what happened to change Lang and hide his own memories from him, but it says nothing. A dust devil spins up near the tent where the men have trodden down the grass and loosened the dry earth.

I watch the dust and wonder what I can do to bring Lang back to himself. If I manage to break the enchantment on him, what will he do when he realizes the position he's in?

Even if these men view him as more than a figurehead, he hasn't been a commander for long. There's little chance that he'd be able to order these soldiers to surrender or return to the capital.

Besides, there are other high-ranking officers here with him who must have their own ideas and thoughts about how to direct these troops. I can imagine resentments among the aristocratic commanders who've served von Kamptz for years, only to have had this young and untried prince thrust suddenly among them—unless they've been enchanted to accept him, as he must have been enchanted to take up the position of prince.

Are there layers of enchantment that tangle across the whole of King Karl's court, like spiderwebs? Marshal Verdugo might know, but I've squandered any chance of ever getting any information out of him.

Knowing the energy that using magic takes from me and Lang, though, that seems unlikely. Von Kamptz would need an army of enchanters, and if he had one, he would surely find some better use for so much magic in this war.

Besides Lang, I know only of the royal astrologer who was in Lang's and Godfather Drosselmeier's stories. He was a friend and companion to Godfather, so he must be an old man now, if he's even still living. Does that mean there is some younger astrologer controlling Lang, as a puppet master pulls the strings to make a painted wooden figure dance?

I shift my weight on my perch and wish I knew more of the details of what was going on in the tent below me. I haven't seen an enchanter or astrologer shadowing Lang, but what does a person using magic look like? Lang is no more a craggy old wizard with a beard and spangled robes than I am.

It's not someone in the camp, then. The whispers among the soldiers pointing to me as the prince's animal familiar haven't pointed out anyone else the men find suspiciously supernatural. Perhaps it isn't even an active control, or he wouldn't have taken notice of me and given me his hand to fly to. Perhaps it's a curse that has changed his mind, as his body was once changed.

I don't like these conclusions. Even with no visible wound on him other than the small slice on his cheek, even though the battle is over—I can't escape the sense that Lang is in danger.

No matter which way I turn things around in my mind, however, I can't see a good way to get him out of here. Certainly I could hop down from this perch, regain my human form, and try to burst into the tent and take him into the dream world with me—all I need is to touch him—but what will happen after that?

Whether his position at the head of these troops is stable or tenuous, it will cause chaos if I make him disappear in front of the other commanding officers. Even if he returns a few minutes later, there will be questions and confusion. If being here is, after all, a deliberate move on his part, then he won't thank me for upsetting his plans yet again.

In the spring, everything was going so well for him under General Carville, until I came and sent the wheels flying off the wagon. I don't understand much of military strategy, but he is here at the defense of the last major barrier to the emperor's army marching into the von Kamptz capital. Or, rather, he was, until I meddled. What will he think when he finds I've sent General Carville's forces slipping around behind him?

If I had fingernails right now, I would be biting them to the quick. Or I would be spinning the ring around my finger, an old anxious habit that began when I had all seven of Lang's rings. Where are the other six? The rings that he should be wearing and isn't?

I must take him out of here. I must speak with him, and yet I don't dare attempt it in this enemy camp. The sun is approaching the horizon. It will be evening, and then night. At some point, he must walk away from this tent for the necessities of his body, or he must sleep. If I pull him into the dream when everyone is sleeping, he won't be missed for a quarter of an hour.

Now I have a plan, and my heart sits easier in my breast. I've waited half the day already. I can wait a little more. But I've also been sitting for too long: my sore muscles are stiffening again. With a last glance at the tent, I stretch my wings and climb up into the sky to circle around the battlefield and the new camp.

There's still a welter of activity among the king's men, all of them going this way and that. The dead have been laid out in long rows while the wounded make their own lines. The horses are corralled together, some obviously captured from the Grand

Army and still wearing tack with their former riders' colors.

I climb higher, so the cluster of red-and-white uniforms shrinks to an ant colony and I can see the wider landscape. I can't go high enough to see the entire country laid out the way it is on the map I gave Keller to return to the general, but I do note the beginnings of the network of roads and streams that run around and into the river. And near the river, I see the small quick shape of a rider galloping toward the camp. Three other horses are in pursuit.

What is this little drama? I spiral down to see.

The rider in front wears the now-familiar red and white. The uniforms of the men following him are even better known to my eye: the green and gold that my brother wears, the same that Lang wore until recently. Three hussars from Fritz's regiment are chasing after a von Kamptz scout. As soon as I see that, I recognize my brother's chestnut stallion, Fox, in the lead among the pursuers.

My first instinct is to dive toward the king's scout. If my brother wants him stopped, then I should help stop him. But he's riding hard toward Lang, making use of his whip to urge his mount on faster. He's carrying some information of deadly importance to von Kamptz, and right now that includes Lang.

I start climbing up through the air currents again, my thoughts racing as quickly as my heart. My brother serves Carville, so he will be protecting something Carville doesn't want his enemy to know. They're coming from the direction of the river where I tried to orchestrate Carville's clash with King Karl at the bridge while Lang went blindly seeking where the Grand Army no longer was.

Suddenly, I've gained enough altitude to see over the line of hills and into the river valley. The valley is full of troops. Tens of thousands of men, far more than I saw marching under Carville in the morning. I fly closer, straining my body for speed and my eyes to see the uniforms and the standards.

None of them are red and white. The von Kamptz standard no longer flies over the bridge. The stone bridge, in fact, is no longer there, but there are three wooden pontoon bridges in its place and the emperor's troops are streaming across them.

This is the news the scout must be carrying. While Lang was leading his men against a small fraction of the Grand Army under Marshal Verdugo, the real battle was happening at his back, and now he is cut off from retreat to the capital.

I cross the hills and drop into the valley until I'm close enough to see what I should have expected: the flags flying where the bridge used to be all show a golden eagle on a deep blue background.

The emperor has arrived.

Chapter Seventeen

Once again I wheel in the sky and fly toward Lang with all possible speed. I pass over the cluster of horses and the three hussars standing around the fallen body of the von Kamptz scout. It's too late to change his fate. I can only push on and hope that whatever winds are near will decide to help me along.

My initial panic passes, and I slow my pace. Even with my extra rest in the dream world, I still need to be careful not to exhaust myself if I want to help Lang.

One thing is certain: I'm no longer waiting until the evening to take him away. He, and the von Kamptz troops with him, are cut off from their capital. They can't retreat. They can only wait for the Grand Army to pick them off at the emperor's leisure.

I saw the dead scout and I saw the fallen men strewn over the field after Verdugo drew the von Kamptz forces away from safety. I can't let Lang suffer that fate.

As soon as I make it back to the camp, I fly directly to the commanders' tent and call as loudly as I can—*kek-kek-kek*—while I circle in the sky. The men look up at me, pointing and calling to one another.

Kek-kek-kek, I cry again. Someone goes into the tent, then Lang and a group of officers emerge and look up. I fly to him, and though his eyes are full of questions, he holds up his hand for me.

"Your Highness," says an older officer beside him. A general? A marshal? He has a canny look that reminds me of Carville, and I don't wait to see what objection he'll voice. I land on Lang's outstretched hand and send my mind to the dream world.

"What is this?" the von Kamptz marshal asks suspiciously, and then he's gone. The camp disappears, and with it, the hard metallic smell of blood. I'd grown so used to it that it's a shock when we're surrounded instead by the sweet scents of the Kingdom of Dolls.

Lang takes a half-step forward, turning to take in our new surroundings. I look too. We aren't beside the lake or in the summerhouse.

No, this time I've brought us into the heart of the nutcracker's capital, into his very castle. We are in the orangery: a room made of glass and stone, filled with green plants and a warm, wet air all its own.

In my hurry, I didn't think clearly about where in the dream world we should go. Instead, my mind latched on to the strongest of my memories about Lang and the Kingdom of Dolls.

The orangery is the place where he and I fought, not long after we first kissed. He told me to wait, and I didn't. Maybe I should have waited now and let events play out between the emperor and King Karl, but I couldn't have left Lang where he was. Not with the Grand Army cutting him off from any safe haven.

"What is this place?" Lang asks. He's finished reviewing the potted fruit trees and the windows left half-open to release the heat which gathers in the glass-walled space. Now he looks at me. "Have you brought me here? Or your master?"

He still thinks that I'm an animal, a creature that can't act by itself and must be directed by someone else. If only he recognized me, this would all be so much easier.

I spread my wings, and he instinctively extends his arm. With room to flutter away from him, I land on a stone bench instead. Is it the same one where I once sat waiting for his return with my heart in my mouth? The plants have been moved around and I can't tell.

It's time for me to transform, but I hesitate. Even if I can't remember the exact bench where I sat, I remember the argument. Lang went to scout through the castle in search of young Drosselmeier and where he'd hidden my niece Clara. Instead of sitting, I went to the doorway and saw when he changed his form from man to mouse.

When he returned, he realized I'd seen his transformation. He could see what I thought of him: the difficulty of bringing together in my mind Dietrich Lang, the man I'd kissed a short time before, and the mouse king, the monster of my childhood nightmares.

I think I understand something of what he must've felt, for now it's my turn to reveal myself as something not quite human. I can't talk with Lang as a hawk. I must return to my human body, but what will he think of me when I do? He has no memory of who I am. To him, I'll be a stranger, a woman with a hawk's golden eyes who has pulled him from one world to another.

Lang steps toward me, then pauses at the potted tree that stands beside the bench. He pulls something from the branches.

"Is this an orange?" he asks, his brow wrinkling. The crust of sugar on the fruit crumbles beneath his touch, white powder falling to the floor as he pulls the fruit open and sniffs it.

If he wanders beyond the orangery, he'll discover the marzipan walls of the castle, the statues of boiled sugar, the slabs of chocolate and gingerbread that make up this part of the dream world. As long as he's cut off from his memories, Lang won't remember all the reasons he has to dislike the nutcracker's magical palace. He won't be aware of the dangers of this place.

He could easily be the soldier that Marshal Verdugo warned of, one who won't want to return from the dream to the waking world. I don't know how, but I have to restore him to himself.

There's no tree to hide behind, as I did with Ensign Keller. None of the potted plants here are large enough, and despite my misgivings, I think I need Lang to see me change. Maybe the sight will trigger something in his mind.

I'm not brave enough, though, to watch for his reaction. I hop down from the bench and turn away as I begin the transformation.

When I pull my trembling body up to sit on the stone floor, Lang has dropped the sugared orange and stands staring at me. I look at him, and my heart sinks. There's no sign he knows me in my human body, either.

He recovers from his surprise, steps back, and draws the sword he carries. It's still a hussar's saber, but this one has gold chasing at the hilt: a prince's weapon.

"What is this?" he demands. "Who are you?"

If our lives were simple, I might have been his wife by now. Instead, I'm preemptively widowed by the tangle of magic and revenge that surrounds him and separates us. I have him with me, safe from the battlefield and close enough to touch, and yet the distance between us is still a yawning gulf.

"Answer me," Lang says. His voice is imperious. Already he is a prince accustomed to his orders being followed without delay or question.

I look up at him, but my throat is too thick with sorrow to form a single word.

He moves forward, keeping his blade leveled at me. "What does your emperor think to gain by taking me away like this?" he asks.

His words divert the heavy flood of painful emotion rolling over me. Does he already know the emperor has cut him off from his uncle's capital? Then I remember I'm dressed in Fritz's old ensign uniform. On top of everything else, he must think I'm part of the Grand Army, who he currently believes to be his enemy. The saber in his hand suddenly seems like a more serious threat.

Any chance of tears evaporates as I evaluate my options. Not only do I need to break this enchantment on him, I must either find a way to do it despite his suspicions of me, or find a way to make him trust me.

"I don't belong to the emperor," I say. "I am my own creature."

"No one is their own creature," he replies immediately. "Everyone answers to someone."

"Who do you answer to, then?" I ask him.

"To the king," he says. "To the lords and the people of the lands we hold."

The way he says the words makes it sound noble: the power of noblesse oblige holding him responsible for and accountable to the people of von Kamptz's kingdom. Is this what his father once felt serving his king, protecting his lands and his people?

The man who stands before me isn't tortured by thoughts of his dead family and driven by an overwhelming desire for revenge. Perhaps he is, by some measure, a better man—but can he really be better if he hasn't chosen to be so, but instead had his thoughts bent in a new direction by an outside magic?

The general's words gnaw at the back of my mind: Lang volunteered for this. What if he asked for this change, to leave behind all the hurt and pain of his past and start over in the bosom of the royal family whose blood he shares?

I find myself echoing back his earlier questions to me. "Who are you? What are you?"

"I am the prince," he says, but his brow crinkles and it sounds more like a question than a statement. "I am the king's nephew. The prince."

I stand, ignoring the point of the sword hovering inches from my breast. If I can't bring him back to himself, I am fatally wounded anyway.

"You are the king's nephew," I tell him. "Your mother was the king's natural sister. Your father was a burgrave. They had seven sons together before the king ordered your father's death and that of all your brothers. You are the last, because your mother sacrificed her life to avenge the others after you were born."

He narrows his eyes and tilts his head to one side, but the

saber doesn't waver. "What tale are you telling?" he asks.

"The truth," I say. "Not a tale, unless it was a tale when you told it to me."

I take a small step forward, until the point of his blade rests against the hollow of my throat. The metal is a cold bite against my skin, a sharp reminder of the consequences this dream conversation will have in the waking world.

"You carried the remembrance of your family with you," I tell him. "Seven rings for seven brothers. Six were on your fingers when I saw you last. The seventh I have."

I lift my hands to show him the ring, and then slide it from my finger. It takes longer than it should. I can't stop the trembling of my body. If he doesn't know the ring, then what will I do? Finally, I hold it out to him. The black smudge covers half the metal now, but there's still a little shine to it. There must be some hope left to recover him.

"You gave it to me," I say, trying to keep my voice steady. "We are bound together, you and I."

His eyes move back and forth between my face and the ring, but I can't read him. He's always been a master at holding his inner thoughts behind a neutral expression. The very blankness of his face now gives me a spark of hope. If he's masking a struggle within himself, then my words must have found some small crack to wiggle through.

"You said I should find you, if you didn't find me," I say. "I learned you were in danger, and I came."

He doesn't say anything, but he takes the ring from me and turns it over in his fingers.

"Where are the other six?" I ask. "Someone has taken them

from you. Someone has taken you from yourself."

Lang looks at the ring, then up at me. His face is a pale mask, nearly as white as the uniform he wears. The red facings are all dark as blood.

I reach up and curl my hand around the end of his blade. It bites into my fingers, but Lang doesn't resist as I move the saber away from my throat and step forward, closing the space between us.

He lets the point of the saber drop, still looking at me with wide eyes.

"Dietrich," I say.

He shudders. "This is a dream."

"What you have been living is the false dream," I say. I wrap my fingers over his hand, where he holds the ring. He trembles under my touch, but he lets me pull it from his palm. "This is a dream, but it is a true one," I say and slip the ring onto his fourth finger.

CHAPTER EIGHTEEN

LANG'S whole body shakes and trembles. His fingers clutch mine, and I grip his hand tightly.

"Dietrich," I say fiercely. "You are Dietrich Lang."

He doesn't reply. Instead, his eyes roll back in his head as he continues to shudder. The saber clatters to the floor as his other hand opens. The spasms are quickly becoming violent.

I step in close. "You are Dietrich Lang," I say again and wrap my arms around him. Just in time, too, for he is falling. We sink onto the flagstones together. He's bigger than me, but not by much, and I'm strong enough now to control his fall.

Despite the heat of the orangery, the stone floor still feels cool. I maneuver him onto his back, holding his head in my lap so he won't hurt himself.

How long does the fit last? A minute? An hour? Time doesn't move regularly in the dream world. It might be a long time simply because I expect it to be. The angle of the light is confused through the thick glass panes and the fronds of palms and pineapples. Some amount of time passes, and Lang quiets.

I wipe the sweat from his face with my sleeve. His officer's bicorn has fallen away, and his hair is a damp tangle. I comb my fingers through it, smoothing his brow until he opens his eyes.

Lang blinks, once, twice, then he says, "Marie."

"Dietrich," I whisper, and then I have to swipe quickly at my eyes before my tears fall into his face.

He reaches up and strokes my cheek. "Oh, my love," he says. "My fierce, sweet love."

He moves to a sitting position and looks around the orangery with sharp eyes. "I see where we are," he says. "Where did you take me from?" Before I can answer, however, his face hardens. "No, I remember," he says. "There was a battle. I fought for von Kamptz, and you were there. An avenging angel."

I reach out to run a finger just above the fresh cut on his face. "I meant to keep you from harm."

"And you did," he says. He catches my hand in his and presses my palm against his cheek. "I have only a scratch, and it will heal. But I gave more to men I should have been fighting alongside with, instead of against."

"Then I did right?" I ask. "I wasn't sure. I thought it could've been part of your plans to be there."

"God, no," he says. He releases me, and his hands go to the stiff gold collar of his jacket. He begins undoing the frog fastenings. "I never wanted this." He waves his hand at the royal uniform. "To be my uncle's puppet? No." He undoes a few buttons of the jacket, then stops and stares at his hands.

"Where are your rings?" I ask.

He turns his hands, looking at his fingers: bare except for the single ring I put on the fourth finger of his left hand.

When he reaches for it, I grab his hand. "Don't. You weren't yourself until you had that ring. Who knows what will happen if you take it off again?"

He looks at the ring, then at me. "Yes," he says. "Safer to leave it for now. The others…" He trails off, his brow crinkling and his mouth settling into a hard line. "They were taken from me, but I will have them back."

He stands and holds out his hand to me. I take it, because my legs are wobbly again, and I need the help to come to my feet.

Lang tucks me close against him, with his arm around my shoulders. I lean into him. At last, we are together—really together. The war is far away, and we can simply be. I breathe deeply, smelling the warm green and sweet citrus scents of the sugared fruits that fill the orangery. This is a reprieve, a chance to redeem the memory of our last meeting here and the fight we had then.

Perhaps Lang is feeling the same, for he leans down and lays a soft kiss on my forehead. "Marie," he says, and my name on his lips is the sweetest sound I've ever heard.

It's not the only sound, though. A rustle of cloth. The click of heeled shoes on stone. Lang's arm tightens on my shoulder as we look around the orangery.

"What's this?" asks a new voice, and young Drosselmeier, the nutcracker, walks through the potted trees towards us.

My first thought is annoyance at the interruption, then relief that he isn't dead. I'd be glad for it, except that I have no wish to see him right now. I didn't want to see him in this place, either, for I hoped he'd find his way back to his parents in Nuremburg.

He must have found the way, as I have, to come and go

between the dream and the waking world as he pleases. Now is not the time to ask, though. Not with Lang rigid beside me and so much left undone in the waking world.

"It seems there is a mouse in my house," Drosselmeier says, and smiles as if he's said something very clever.

A titter of laughter follows. He's not alone. There are four women moving through the orangery around him, beautiful and dressed as richly as princesses. The memory of my long-ago first visit to this place comes back, murky with disuse. Four princesses in the nutcracker's palace, whom he introduced as his sisters.

Lang hasn't said anything in return to Drosselmeier's taunt. He hasn't even moved, though his hand grips my shoulder almost painfully tight. When I glance away from the nutcracker and his strange entourage, I belatedly see that Lang isn't merely tense in readiness against a potential threat. He is frozen in panic.

I put my own arm around his waist. What is he thinking of right now, with the nutcracker unexpectedly before him? The death of his mother? The bloody battle when young Drosselmeier took his brothers' crowns from him?

The princesses giggle again, hiding their faces behind ivory fans. Something is odd about their appearance. I hold onto Lang, and Lang holds onto me, and I stare at the four women and their moving fans. Finally, I realize that they're all identical, like a set of porcelain dolls with the same painted face.

"Marie," Lang whispers. "Get us out of here."

He's right. Whatever is going on with Drosselmeier and these doll-princesses, I don't want to find out right now.

The nutcracker steps forward, his scarlet frock coat flaring around his slender body, and I think *wake*—

Back to the waking world, to the camp I took Lang from, with the von Kamptz standard fluttering in the breeze and the dust and the blood and the officers. I open my mouth on a yawn, my ears pop, and we are away and gone from the orangery and the nutcracker's realm.

Men surround us in a wall of red-and-white uniforms. There are gasps and shouts at our sudden appearance in their midst.

Why did I come back here? Anywhere else would have been better, but I'm too tired now to think where else. Lang is holding me up, our bodies still pressed close, but there is the officer in front of us—the marshal who was suspicious of me as a hawk.

As usual, I've made the wrong decision. I have to get us out before—

The von Kamptz marshal doesn't join in the shouting. Instead, he raises a pistol and shoots. There is a loud report and immediately pain and pain and pain—

Lang is shouting and the men around us are shouting—

The summerhouse, if I can just—

My vision goes black around the edges, but the shouting stops and there is only Lang, repeating my name.

He lays me down on the sofa. His hands are red with blood, which must be mine? Everything is dark again and—

"Marie," Lang says, his voice sharp and dark with emotion.

His face is right in front of mine, his eyes wide and intense. The most handsome man I've ever seen. I want to just lie here and look at him until the end of time.

"Marie, you fierce, beautiful creature," he says. "Don't you dare leave me like this."

No, not like this, my love. Why am I the one bleeding? I thought I would be saving him. Trudy even gave me the laudanum and the needle and thread in case I had to stitch him up. And now—

"Marie," he says again, as if he can tether me to life with just the power of his voice.

I'm so tired, but he looks so unhappy. I want to reach for him. I should at least tell him about the supplies Trudy gave me. "Laudanum," I say, or try to.

He's stroking my hair, I think, but he pauses and leans in closer. I try to lift the arm that hasn't dissolved into pain and point to the necklace and the little pouch Trudy made.

"Needle and thread," I tell him.

He moves back, his face swimming away from me in a gray-purple sea of light. I feel him fumble with the terrible, interminable fastenings of my ensign's jacket and then he pulls out the pouch. Once he has it, he only looks at the contents and shakes his head. He doesn't know what it is, or he doesn't know what to do with it, or maybe it just isn't enough to save me.

That's all right, though, because at least I've saved him. I close my eyes on that thought.

"No," Lang says. There's a new pressure-pain as he slaps my cheek and forces my eyes open. "Stay with me, Marie." He sets the pouch aside. "If not for me, then for everyone else who loves and needs you."

I think of my brother, my sister, the rest of my family, my friends—Trudy, who sewed the little pouch and wanted so much to help.

If Trudy were here, she would know what to do, but I've never brought her into the dream world. I should have brought her with me.

Trudy will help me, if she looks up from her sewing and finds herself not in her parents' parlor, but in the summer-house—

"Marie!" Lang says. "Marie!"

But his voice fades, and everything is dark.

Chapter Nineteen

"Do something for her," Lang demands.

"I've already done all I can," replies Trudy's voice.

Lang makes a sound of frustration, and Trudy continues. "I took out the bullet, but the bones are shattered. There's nothing more to be done"—she pauses, and I hear the creak of floorboards, as if one of them is pacing the room—"except to take off her arm." She stops again, and now there is dead silence.

"No," Lang says, while I'm still working out what it would mean to take off my arm. No arm, no wing, no flight. I'll be trapped on the ground forever. I don't want to be trapped.

"If the wound goes bad," Trudy says, "it will kill her. You know it. You must have seen it happen to others."

"No." This time Lang's voice breaks on the single word.

Where is he? I open my eyes and see a whitewashed ceiling above me. I have to concentrate very hard to turn my head to the side, but there they are: my best friend sitting wearily in a straight-backed chair while my lover paces.

"She'll never fly again," Trudy says, "but at least she'll be alive."

Lang reaches the end of the small white room and smashes his fist against the wall. The plaster cracks and dribbles to the floor.

"Stop that," Trudy snaps at him. "This is no easier for me than for you, but I'm not going to break my hands over it."

"This is all my fault," he says. "It should've been me. I swore an oath to protect her." He turns toward me, meets my gaze, and rushes over. "Marie," he says, reaching out to touch my face.

I can barely feel his fingers. They must have given me the laudanum after all, for my body is flat and numb, as if I'm not quite connected to it.

My thoughts, too, scatter like a flock of songbirds beneath a stooping hawk. I struggle to catch one and hold onto it. *Hawk?*

"You brought Mademoiselle Wendelstern to us," Lang says. "She dressed your wound." He hesitates, then says, "You will recover, and all will be well."

But all will not be well. Not if I am to lose my wing.

"Hawk," I say. I want to fly.

His mouth twitches, then he flattens his expression, hiding his emotions. Ah, my love, always with so many worries weighing him down. I want to fly with him, the way we do in my dreams, with no earthly cares. I would shift right now, if I had the strength.

Trudy appears next to Lang. "Don't try to move," she warns me.

There was something—I almost had it, but her words distract me and my mind can't catch whatever thought I was close to grasping.

"You will be a hawk again," Lang says, and that's it—that's

the thought.

"Hawk," I say. I need to be a hawk. I clutch at the thought, dig my talons into it so it can't get away. *I need to be a hawk.* "Change me," I say.

"No," Trudy says. "You've only just stopped bleeding, Mariechen."

I've caught the thought that says I must transform, but the why of it is another thing, and that has escaped me. I can't explain it to them, but the overwhelming sense that I need the transformation buoys me up like a warm air current. I'm too weak to do it myself, though. "Change me," I say again. "Dietrich."

"You will change yourself," he says. "When you are better. But you must rest now." He strokes my face and leans in to brush a kiss on my forehead. I catch the glitter of unshed tears in his eyes. Then he backs away, and Trudy is there instead, tipping something into my mouth. I swallow reflexively.

"Sleep now, Mariechen," she says, and she doesn't promise that I will be better, or that I will fly again.

More laudanum, I think, and then I don't think, but perhaps I sleep, or perhaps I don't? I can't remember closing my eyes, but I open them, and Lang is asleep in the chair with his head lolled to one side at an uncomfortable looking angle.

I close my eyes, trying to take stock of my body. I am lying on my back somewhere flat and hard. A table? My feet are cold. I try to feel if there is a blanket over me, and there is the pain that has been my constant companion. Only my left arm moves when I tell it; only my left hand feels the rough-warm texture of wool over me.

I was trapped in a wool blanket. It wrapped around my

wings, and I couldn't fly. I couldn't get to Lang when I needed to help him. Where is the general? What is he going to do to Lang? Will he shoot him? Will he shoot me? I have to get out of this wool prison and fly. I have to take Lang with me.

Then Lang is with me. "Be easy, liebling," he says. He takes my left hand in both of his and kisses my cold fingers. "I'm here. We won't be separated again."

"Carville," I say, but already I'm forgetting what was important about him. He's not here. Lang is, and I want to lift my hand and wipe away the tired lines around his eyes. My arm doesn't move when it should, though.

Is it even there? Without it, I won't be able to fly. I try to tug my left hand from Lang's grasp and reach across to my other shoulder. It must be there. It couldn't hurt so much and not be there.

"What about Carville?" Lang asks, but I have no idea what he's talking about.

"My wing," I say, and his face shutters so quickly that I know something must be very wrong. Am I dying, then? Will we never get to fly together? I want to fly. I need to fly. If I can just transform again, everything will be better. "Change me."

He shakes his head, and I can feel the pressure of his hands tighten around mine. He swallows once, twice, before he answers. "You're delirious," he says softly. "It's the pain and the laudanum together."

Probably he's right, but the feeling grows into a certainty: *I must be a hawk*. If I'm dying anyway, then let me die with wings. I will spend eternity in the skies, watching over those I love. "Make me a hawk," I insist.

He looks at me, still as stone. I would think that time had

stopped altogether, except that a single teardrop spills over and tracks down his stubbled cheek.

"Please," I say.

He takes a deep, shuddering breath. "Very well," he says. He lets go of my hand, leans forward, and kisses me again.

When he presses his lips to mine, it feels like goodbye, but I'm not ready for goodbye. I lift my good hand to the back of his neck and keep him close. "We will fly," I say. "Together."

He doesn't reply. He brushes his mouth over mine once more, then draws back with a last caress over my cheek. He squeezes his eyes shut over his tears, and I want to tell him that this isn't it, this isn't the end, but he's done as I asked and my body is shifting.

It's painful, but it's a welcome, familiar pain after the throbbing wrongness of my shattered shoulder. My bones reform. My muscles knit together. My skin flows unbroken over my body, my clothing becomes a part of my plumage.

I struggle weakly against the blanket that covers me. It is lifted, and Lang looks down at me. I open my wings as soon as I'm free. Joy and relief flood through me, for they do open—my wings, both of them. My right shoulder joint twinges, but it is there, just as it ought to be.

Lang stares down at me. "Oh," he says. "Oh, god, Marie." Tears are streaming down his face, and I know he expected that he'd killed me with the transformation. He holds up his hands, as if he would embrace me, but I'm the wrong shape for holding now. Instead, he modifies the gesture and gives me one hand to be a perch.

I step up onto the wide base of his thumb. With his other hand, he wipes his face and then strokes my body. Without another word, he lifts me and walks to the door.

Now that I have awareness beyond my pain, I see that we're in a facsimile of the room in the Wendelsterns' house where Trudy's father conducts surgeries. When we pass out of the whitewashed room, though, we are in the summerhouse.

Lang carries me down the hall, past Trudy asleep on the divan, and upstairs to the bedchamber we shared before. Very gently, he sets me down on the carpet that covers the floor.

"Do I change you again?" he asks.

I bob my head. *Yes.*

He kneels in front of me, acting without hesitation this time. When the transformation is finished, he gathers me in his arms and carries me the few steps to the bed. There is no undressing, or even pulling back the bedclothes: the moment we lay down, we fall into the dreamless sleep of utter exhaustion.

Chapter Twenty

I WAKE with something tickling my neck. After a moment, I realize it's the curling ends of my own cropped hair, moving with Lang's breath. He lies at my back with his arm wrapped tightly around me.

I tuck my arm against Lang's and snuggle more closely into him. He sighs and nuzzles the nape of my neck. We're in the dream world, where there are no armies marching anywhere, and no enemies to raise sword or gun against us. Everything is warm and comfortable and safe, and I want it to stay this way as long as possible.

For a time, I float in that place between sleeping and waking, as effortless as soaring in the sky with a good air current beneath me. But thoughts of the events that brought us to this place intrude. Soldiers screaming, crying, fighting, dying. Curses and enchantments, bullets and battlefields.

Lang and I are still wearing the uniforms of opposing armies as we lie together. Lang is, at least. I can feel the stiff gold braid at the cuffs of his jacket, but my jacket has disappeared somewhere and I'm wearing a loose shirt with the breeches of my ensign's uniform. The buoying current disappears, and I can't find my way back into sleep.

My restlessness wakes Lang. The moment he comes into awareness, his muscles tense and his breath goes quick and shallow. He curves his body around mine, making himself into a protective shell over me.

I twist beneath him and cup my hands to his face. "We're safe," I tell him. "I'm safe." I repeat the words until his breathing slows again.

"Marie," he says. "I thought—"

He stops, not willing to finish the sentence.

"I know," I say. I wrap my arms around him, and slowly he relaxes against me, burying his face in my neck. I stroke his hair and his back, wishing it was his bare skin beneath my fingers instead of the von Kamptz uniform. The last time we shared this bed, clothing wasn't involved. We're safe, and we're in a bed. Shouldn't we make the most of it?

Lang murmurs something against my skin and kisses my ear. I shift my hips, feeling the pleasurable weight of him settling against me. Waking next to him felt good, but this feels even better. As I arch up into his touch, though, my mind is still sorting through recent events, and a sudden thought washes over me like cold rain.

The nutcracker. In the palace with the doll-princesses.

I've been treating the dream world as if it were entirely my own, but we're not alone in it.

"Dietrich." I wriggle beneath him. "Wait."

He rolls off of me immediately. "Did I hurt you?" he asks.

"Are you still injured?"

Am I? "No," I say. There's some remnant soreness, but it's all in the muscles. I think Trudy said something about broken bones, but nothing feels broken now. That's not what worries me. "We saw the nutcracker in the palace. What if he knows we are here?"

What if it wasn't Lang he meant when he said there was a mouse, but me? I've been coming to this far corner of the Kingdom of Dolls for months now. I always assumed that I was alone here, except for my accidental guest in General Carville. But what if the nutcracker has been here all along? I don't know what it means, but the thought leaves me unsettled.

Lang sits up. "Not just him," he says. "But the princess. Or copies of her."

"They were dolls," I say. "Like the others we saw in the capital before."

He shakes his head. "They had my cousin's face. It's too much to be a coincidence." He runs his hands through his hair, leaving tufts sticking straight up from his head. "You asked who took the other rings from me," he says. "It was my cousin."

"Your cousin?" I ask. I sit up, too. "The princess?"

"She's more than a princess," Lang says. "The royal astrologer is dead, but she inherited his library. I destroyed some of the books when I returned to von Kamptz's palace before, but there were others. She must have gone looking, as I did, for information about what was done to her, and she learned—" He stops and spreads his hands wide. "I don't know what she learned, exactly, but enough to take the rings and hide part of my mind from me. I should have burned the entire library when I had the chance."

"You destroyed books?" I ask. I think of Petra's friend, collecting stories to make books. Books are precious, expensive things.

"The information in them destroyed my family," Lang says. "I didn't want the same to be done to anyone else."

"Oh," I say. I've wondered before why he didn't spend more time with the astrologer's library and the knowledge it must have held. Why didn't he learn more magic? But now I think of how he speaks about magic and his reactions on coming to the Kingdom of Dolls. "You don't actually like magic," I say slowly. "Do you?"

He shakes his head and pulls me close, so I can lean against him and he can put his arm around me. "When magic came into your childhood, it brought you joy and wonder," he says, measuring out the words carefully. "For me, magic broke everything before I ever knew what it was." He sighs and adds, "It was the same for my cousin, and even for young Drosselmeier. Magic is something that was done to us, not an adventure we were offered."

"Oh," I say again. "But you learned to fly."

"I did," he agrees. "And I enjoy being a hawk, but not as much as you do, I think." He kisses the top of my head. "I'm glad I could give it to you as a gift. And I suppose I must also admit a debt to young Drosselmeier, who made magic an adventure for you rather than a curse. Otherwise, you might not have come for me."

I put my head on his chest and my arms around him as I consider what he's told me. It's true: when I first met the nutcracker, magic was the dream world, and the Kingdom of Dolls a realm of marzipan castles and joyful toys. But for the others, for Lang and Paula Maria and young Drosselmeier, magic was curses that changed their forms and made them into monsters.

Lang found the key to unlock his humanity in the astrologer's books. The princess's curse was broken when young Drosselmeier accidentally transferred it to himself, and I broke Drosselmeier's curse when I declared my love for him in a moment when I believed I did. At least, I assumed I'd broken his curse, for the nutcracker doll disappeared and he appeared at my parents' Christmas party in human form. But he's still here in the dream world with those strange living images of the princess.

"Young Drosselmeier was supposed to break the curse and marry your cousin," I say. "Perhaps he made those copies of her to be his companions in this realm."

"That could be so," Lang admits. "I don't know if she's aware of the Kingdom of Dolls, but it's certainly possible."

"How could she not know of it?" I ask.

Before Lang can answer, there is a soft rap on the door. I hear Trudy clear her throat. "Lieutenant Lang?" she calls tentatively.

Lang and I exchange guilty looks, though we haven't managed to get up to anything even vaguely scandalous. Then I remember Trudy doesn't know I've been healed by the magic reworking my body. What must she have imagined to find me gone from the table in the surgery?

I disentangle myself from Lang, push off the bed, and go to pull open the door. "Here I am," I say.

She stares at me as if seeing a ghost. "Marie?" she asks. Then, "Marie!" She throws her arms around me, but releases me just as quickly. "What are you doing up? Sit down. Lie down. Let me look at your shoulder."

Lang moves out of the way as she leads me back to the bed. I sit and let her slip my shirt down around my right shoulder. She runs her hands over my skin. There's a smooth, white circle on the front of my shoulder, like a strange coin embedded there: a reminder of the price paid for my arm, my wing, my life.

Trudy stares at it, her face pale and her eyes wide. She looks up at me, then turns to Lang, who stands beside us, also looking at the mark on my shoulder. "What did you do?" she asks him.

"He changed me to a hawk," I say. "The magic remade me."

Trudy sits down on the bed beside me. "I didn't know it could do that," she says.

"Neither did I," Lang says. He meets my gaze and says quietly, "I thought if it was your last wish to be a hawk, I couldn't refuse you."

There is a long silence while Lang and I look at each other, and I try not to cry. Then, finally, Trudy says, "What now?"

CHAPTER TWENTY-ONE

TOGETHER Lang and I tell each other and Trudy what we've been through: the enchantment the princess put on him, his actions at the head of the von Kamptz army, my visit with General Carville and Marshal Verdugo, how I pulled Lang away, and how we saw the nutcracker with the princess.

I leave out my last conversation with Ensign Keller, remembering his hesitation before he asked me to transform his body. I don't want to tell his secrets unnecessarily, even to Trudy.

If he survived the day's action, and I can find him again, then I'll tell Lang about the help I promised to the ensign. I think of my brother and his fellows standing around the fallen von Kamptz scout, and hope that Keller hasn't met a similar fate.

"If young Drosselmeier knew you were here," Trudy says, waving her hand to indicate the summerhouse, "then he could've come here any time. If he hasn't, then either he doesn't know, or he doesn't care to bother you."

We've moved to the main room on the first floor, where

we can look out the windows across the lake. The nutcracker's capital looms on the far side of the rose water lake, but there is no flotilla coming over the water towards us.

If the nutcracker can influence this world as I've found myself able to, however, there is nothing that would stop him from appearing in this room the instant he wanted to. Perhaps Trudy is right about young Drosselmeier, but that still leaves the question of the princess.

"If Princess Paula Maria could come into the Kingdom of Dolls," I say, "then Drosselmeier wouldn't need the doll-princesses with him. And he wouldn't have needed to bring me here either."

"That is sensible," Lang agrees. "But even if she can't come here, we must go to her. I will get my rings back, and I will see von Kamptz fall before the emperor."

"What about me?" Trudy asks. She looks between me and Lang. "I don't want to confront kings and princesses, but I'd rather you didn't leave me here."

All she must do is wake, and she'll be safe at home. But will she wake in her own home? This is her first visit between worlds, after all. I remember when I brought Lang and Clara back from the dream. We ended up in the forest half an hour's ride from our city, and in the middle of winter. No, I definitely can't send Trudy back alone.

"We'll take you home," I say. "Then we'll pass through the dream world again to where we need to go." I look to Lang, who nods.

"We've been here for a few days," he says. "So it will be evening in the waking world. Perhaps we can get you home before dark, Mademoiselle Wendelstern, and save you some trouble."

Before we leave, Lang goes upstairs and returns dressed in his familiar hussar lieutenant's uniform, dark green with yellow braid. He brings me a fresh ensign's jacket as well, for the one that was my brother's must be bloody and torn somewhere in the surgery room. The new jacket is clean and unstained, and even cut a little differently, for it fits better over my breasts when I fasten it up.

When we're ready, I take Lang's hand in one of mine and grasp Trudy's with the other. Then I set my mind to the forest just outside the city wall, the way the light slants through the trees as the sun sets, when Trudy and I might be hurrying home from the day's hunt. I yawn, and yawn again, and Trudy says, "Oh!"

I open my eyes, and we're exactly where I wanted to be: the place where the forest path we've taken so often meets with the road. Lang looks around and sniffs the air. Trudy clings tightly to my hand, then takes a deep breath. "Will you walk me to the edge of the trees?"

"Of course," I say.

Lang falls a few paces behind us. I can feel his presence at my back, watchful and waiting.

Trudy glances over her shoulder at him, then leans close to me as we walk. "When I—when you weren't there—" She stops and begins again. "I've seen it a few times, when Father hasn't been able to save a person, and someone who loved them goes mad with grief." She squeezes her fingers in mine and continues, speaking in low tones. "I thought you were dead, Mariechen, and I would have to take you—your body—from him."

She flings her arms around me in a fierce hug. I hug her back, both of us shaking.

"I'm glad it wasn't so," I whisper.

"Me too," she replies.

She releases me from her embrace, wipes her eyes, and takes my hand again. We walk on, with Lang still keeping a respectful distance behind us.

When we come to the edge of the trees, Trudy stops again. I can see on her face that she has something else to say, and, after a moment, it comes out in a rush.

"He loves you," she says. "And you love him. And your brother—I thought I loved your brother, but I don't. Not like that."

"Oh, Trudy," I say, ready to claim that Fritz will notice her someday, but she shakes her head.

"No," she says. "I'm not sad. It's freeing. And hopeful, I think, because I wish your brother well, but somewhere out there is someone who will care for me so much more than he ever would."

"I hope you find that person," I say.

"And I hope you and Lieutenant Lang find a way to end this war," she says.

We hug once more, then she walks out of the trees. Lang moves to stand beside me, and we watch as she crosses the field. The city wall is lit by torches against the warm, gathering night.

"I would expect no less from a friend of yours," Lang says, "but I think Mademoiselle Wendelstern a remarkable young woman."

"It's too bad Fritz will never realize it," I say.

"Your brother?" Lang asks. He raises an eyebrow and looks at the city gate again. Trudy has gone through now, safe behind the high stone and earthen walls.

"She's not waiting for him," I say quickly.

"I see," he says, and I think he's about to say something else, but he only shakes his head. "How are you feeling?" he asks. "We must go between worlds twice more, and then we may need to fly."

"It's easiest to wake from the dream," I tell him. "I'm not too tired." I take his hand and lead him back into the darkness under the trees.

I want to take us back to the summerhouse, to sleep there before we continue with what we must do, but it's stained with memories of blood and fear, and the looming unknown of where the nutcracker is and what his intentions might be. What was once my refuge can be no longer.

Instead of walking through to the summerhouse, I take us to another part of the dream world. The twilight around us shimmers and reforms, and damp gravel shifts beneath our feet.

"Ah," Lang says. "The beach."

We're beside the rose water lake, on the pebbled shore where the swans brought us after the clockwork ship that first carried us into the dream sank. Somewhere nearby is the rounded island of licorice rushes and the nest where I slept that night, but it's already too dark to see much of anything.

We feel our way to where a few huge logs of driftwood rest above the waterline and climb up to sit side by side on one of them. Lang puts his arm around me, and we sit in the dark, listening to the ceaseless murmur of the water.

I still don't feel as tired as I'd expected to. Having Lang at my side gives me strength, even knowing that we must soon go to the battlefield. I feel fully ready to fly, but then I doubt myself. What's wrong with me that even as I was on the edge of death, I wanted to trade my human form for an animal's?

I lean into Lang and hold the words in my mouth as long as I can, but once I've thought them, they can't help but come out. "Dietrich?" I ask. "Are we still human?"

He's been tracing some unknown pattern on the surface of the wood with his free hand, but he stops. I bite my tongue, wishing I hadn't asked. I used to think he was a monster, and he knows it.

"We've spoken of this before," he says finally. "When I was the one doubting. You told me I was human, because I chose to be a man rather than an animal."

"But I don't always choose to be human," I whisper. "I've become a hawk every chance I could since we were parted, and…" I trail off, hesitating to say the next part, even here in the quiet dark. "I've hunted and killed, and I would do it again. I *will* do it again."

He goes still, then asks, "What have you hunted?"

"Rabbits, mostly. Some game birds. And"—I hesitate, then remind myself that he must already know what I did during the battle—"and Marshal Verdugo, on the battlefield."

"Setting aside the marshal for now," Lang says, "what have you done with the rabbits and the birds?"

I blink. "Taken them to my family. Some I gave to Trudy for her family."

He leans his head close to mine, pressing his lips to my temple. "Marie, my love, you took me from a smoking, stinking, bloody battlefield. In a little while, we'll return there and be surrounded again by the dead that men leave in far greater numbers and to far less purpose than a hawk hunting to feed her family. I don't know that you should necessarily hold humanity up too highly."

"And the marshal?" I ask. "I didn't kill him, but I hurt him as much as I could. I was so angry to find them marching toward you, instead of around."

"Marshal Verdugo has commanded soldiers to do far worse," Lang says. "He made his own decisions that led him to be there on the battlefield. And I can't say you were wrong to protect me." He kisses my forehead again. "We may be more than human, Marie, but we're definitely not less. And if you were anything but what you are, neither of us would be alive today."

We shift to the widest end of the log, where the tree's bare roots spread up and to the sides, like great wings of pale wood. Lang leans against the roots, and I lean back into him, nestled between his outstretched legs with his arms around me. We talk until we grow too sleepy to continue, then we doze for a while.

When I wake, the shell pink moon has risen over the lake. It adds a pearly glow to the night landscape. A little way down the shore, I see the forms of the swans who live on the lake, sleeping like snow drifts on the beach.

I put my hands over Lang's where they rest at my waist. The night air has cooled, but not so much that I feel cold, especially with our two bodies together.

He shifts his hands to cover mine, surrounding me in a full-body embrace. "Are you rested?" he asks. "We should go. Things can happen quickly between armies, even in the night."

I sigh and disentangle myself from him to slide down from the log. My backside is numb from sitting so long, but I stretch, then take Lang's hand when he comes to stand next to me. "Where do we go, though?" I ask. "It has to be somewhere I can picture. I can't take us to the von Kamptz palace."

"How about some*one*, instead of some*where*?" Lang suggests. "We don't know where the different troops will be compared to the afternoon when we left, and I don't want either of us to be shot when we appear."

"But who do we trust not to shoot us?" I ask. "Fritz? He won't be alone."

I hear the wry smile in Lang's voice as he answers. "I know you have no love for him, but I think it must be General Carville. He won't shoot me until he's had the chance to interrogate me. And he won't shoot you, because then I won't tell him anything."

I think of the spring night when I lay trapped in my hawk's body and wrapped in a wool blanket while Carville forced out Lang's confession of his parentage. That was before the general knew that I was the hawk. I don't entirely share Lang's trust in his former commander's benevolence, but I don't have a better option. The general will be close to the river, at least, and he might even be in the capital already.

"Will you talk to him?" I ask. "Or will we fly straight away for your uncle?"

"We must talk to him," Lang says. "We may need his information as much as he needs ours."

"Very well," I say. I wish that we could have gone home when Trudy did, but I understand by now that Lang won't rest until he's finished this thing with his uncle. We'll go to the general.

Chapter Twenty-Two

I SQUEEZE Lang's hand in mine and picture General Carville, tired after the long day's march and battle, the way he takes off his glasses and massages the bridge of his nose. I yawn, and Lang yawns, and when I open my eyes again, there are uniformed men huddled around a table, peering at a map lit by a lamp. They don't notice us immediately, for we're at the edge of the group.

"Hold tight to me," Lang murmurs. "We may need to return quickly to the dream, but wait until I give the sign."

I nod and look around. There's no tent this time. We're in what would be a ballroom under more peaceful circumstances. The chandeliers have been pulled down. They make strange knobbly shapes amid pooled fabric that must have been heavy drapes for the windows and doors, which are now open to the night. From the darkness outside, a distant high keening reaches my ears.

The men are all listening to one of the officers, who waves his hands animatedly as he speaks about troop movements. He has a sharp nose and deep, intense eyes that draw me in even though he doesn't look in our direction.

I pull my gaze from him and look at the other men clustered together. There is Marshal Verdugo, now with a sling on his arm as well as the bandage on his head. By uniform, there are two other marshals here, and two generals, one of whom is General Carville. The officer who holds their attention wears a strangely unmarked uniform, and I can't judge his rank. There are a few other soldiers hovering about, obviously aides to the great men.

Ensign Keller is next to Carville, taking notes in a small book. It's Keller who first looks away from the speaker and catches sight of me and Lang.

"That's him," Lang says into my ear, as Keller's mouth drops open and he hurries toward us. "The emperor."

I look at the intense man whose uniform has none of the gold ostentation that Lang was dressed in to be a von Kamptz prince. *That* is the emperor? The man whose ambition and military genius has rearranged half the world? But yes: even if his clothing doesn't trumpet the fact, I do know his face. His likeness has been in the newspapers, on engravings and plates and a dozen other things that can be sold as memorabilia of these strange years of war.

Keller tugs on my arm. "What are you doing here?" he hisses.

I look up at Lang. "Do we go?" I was ready to take on King Karl, but the emperor? I never expected to encounter the emperor even once in my entire life. We should forget the idea of talking with Carville and run out the door, fly through the open windows, retreat into the dream.

But Lang shakes his head. "No. Not yet," he says, and then

it's too late for us to slip out quietly, for more heads turn our way.

The emperor looks up from the map and pins us beneath his gaze. I can hardly breathe with those eyes turned on me. It is as if he looks into my very heart and sees every secret there, as if in an instant he has weighed my significance and decided my place in his plans, along with everyone else in the room.

"The elusive von Kamptz prince," he says, and all my instincts scream *Run! Fly!*

"Hold," Lang whispers to me, so I hold tightly to his hand as he says, loud enough for the whole room to hear, "I am no prince."

Will he kneel to the emperor, as he once did before General Carville? Would it convince this man that we are no threat? But Lang doesn't kneel. As the emperor steps towards us, Lang remains straight and tall. He doesn't bend or salute. With his words, he's denied his royal claim, but his posture says otherwise.

"And this must be the equally elusive Sturm," the emperor says.

"Sir," I say, and my voice squeaks on the word. I try again. "Yes, Your Majesty."

The emperor stops two paces away and clasps his hands behind his back. "You have been busy," he says. "I've heard a number of reports about both of you." He nods toward Carville, who looks displeased but unsurprised to see us, and Marshal Verdugo, whose face says clearly that he knows I'm responsible for his newest wounds.

Lang says nothing to that, so I keep my mouth shut as well.

"Have you come to claim your kingdom?" the emperor asks.

His tone is mild, as if Lang had forgotten a glove after a game of cards last week and only just now remembered to stop by for it.

"No," Lang says. "I have come for my uncle."

The emperor's eyes gleam in the candlelight. "And what will you do with him?"

"I will see the end of his dynasty," Lang says.

"Your Imperial Majesty," one of the unknown marshals begins, then falls silent as the emperor holds up a hand.

"To end a royal line is no simple thing," he says, and the words are not mere platitude, but full of the history of his own rise to power and the overthrow of the dynasty he has replaced. There are still heirs to that line, I think, taking refuge in the courts that haven't yet fallen before him. "Especially when you are a part of it," he adds.

His eyes flick to me, and I know he hasn't missed Lang's and my hands tightly clasped together. What calculation has he made from that fact? That Lang might father children who will seek to reclaim the von Kamptz throne?

"I am no prince," Lang says again. "Nor would I be a king. Von Kamptz renounced me until he had a use for me, and I renounce him in turn."

The emperor's gaze returns to me, but he speaks to Lang. "You led von Kamptz's army," he says. "I've even heard you were promised to marry the princess."

Marry his cousin? My heart jolts painfully, but Lang squeezes my fingers and the feeling of panic passes quickly. Lang won't marry his cousin. To anyone who knows a fraction of their history, the idea is patently ridiculous.

"My mind was not my own," Lang says. "Magic was used to coerce me."

The emperor is still watching me, and I think suddenly that I'm the one he's testing. Lang is known to Carville, and what the general knows he must've told his emperor.

Lang has announced his intentions and his loyalties before, and never wavered from them except while the princess had enchanted him. But they don't know me, or what I want now that I've found Lang. This talk of dynasties and marriages is for me, either to loosen the bond that ties me to Lang, or simply to see what I might give away in my reactions.

What information has the emperor drawn from me while I've been unaware? I don't know the pattern of his thoughts any more than he does mine.

"I cannot help but wonder what magic acts on you now," the emperor says thoughtfully, and another piece of this puzzle slides into place.

Even after all the secrets that have been revealed with such disastrous consequences, they haven't learned that Lang has his own magic. I mentioned it to Keller, but the ensign has his own secrets to keep and he must've kept the information to himself.

When Carville interrogated Lang, he gave up the information of his blood relation to von Kamptz, but not what he learned from the royal astrologer's library. Meanwhile, they know that I move between worlds and forms, but they don't know how or why I've formed a connection with Lang. I could almost laugh, if I weren't aware of how unwise such a reaction would be.

"There's no magic on me now," Lang says. "I'm free to think my own thoughts and to choose both my own actions and my own companions in them." He takes a small but deliberate step closer to me. "Where is my uncle?"

The emperor stares at us for a long time, with his lips slightly pursed and his eyes full of whirring, unreadable thoughts. The marshals, the generals, and the aides-de-camp all stand in expectant silence, their gazes moving between us and their commander.

If he says the word, they'll rush to try and capture us, magic or no magic. Then I'll pull us back to the dream world, where we'll sort out any unwelcome visitors and take time to recover before we can try again. If I end up with half the emperor's inner circle in the Kingdom of Dolls, it will send ripples of chaos through both the dream and the waking world that I can't even begin to imagine.

Maybe we should go now, before they come at us, but Lang has given me no sign. He's still waiting for an answer from the emperor. Even without bringing a stray general or marshal with us, returning to the dream would still be time lost.

I bite the inside of my cheek, wishing I could see a simple solution—but there's never a simple solution to anything. Every action leads to a cascade of other movements, just as the turn of a key in a clockwork sets one cog turning two cogs, which turn three more, and eventually a whole host of others are in motion. Once, long ago, King Karl asked his royal astrologer to make Lang's mother and her family disappear, and now here we are.

"Karl has fled," the emperor says finally. "I hold his capital."

"If you have the map I gave General Carville, then you'll have no trouble in finding him," I say.

He looks at me, and I recognize him as one predator knows another. This man knows what it is to grasp and rip and tear and come away bloody. But where I am a hawk, the emperor is an eagle: big enough to knock me from the sky. This is a dangerous game we're playing, Lang and I.

"The question, mademoiselle, is not whether I will find him," says the emperor. "The question is what I do with him when he is found. Shall I make a new treaty with him, when he's broken the old? Shall I exile him? Strip him of his lands and titles? Shall I make his daughter my wife, and his heirs my own?"

"It was the princess who put the influence of magic on me," Lang says. "If you let her close to you, you may find yourself acting for the interests of von Kamptz, rather than the Empire."

The emperor arches an eyebrow. "Is that so?" he asks. "I will keep that in mind. I'd like an enchanting wife, but perhaps not so enchanting as that."

A few of the officers allow themselves small smiles at the emperor's witticism, but I think instead of Lang's words about the effect magic has had on his life, and that of the princess: "Magic broke everything."

Princess Paula Maria was promised to whomever could break her curse, but there was no marriage after young Drosselmeier accidentally took the curse on himself. How many times since then has she been dangled as a prize as part of her father's political maneuvering? She's no longer cursed with a doll's body, but from what I know about the life of a princess, she might as well be nothing more than an ornament passed from one powerful man to another.

If her father hadn't been so jealous of his sister's sons and the line of succession to his throne, then her life—and mine—would have gone very differently.

"As for the king," Lang says, "I wouldn't expect him to keep to any treaty you can't hold him to by force."

"Very well," the emperor says. The officers around him straighten up and prick their ears at the tone of his voice, like a pack of hounds who know the hunt will soon begin. "I shall allow you to seek Karl. I have men pursuing him, of course, but if you bring him to me, then I will consider it a service to the empire great enough to erase the treason you committed, as you claim, under the influence of your cousin's enchantment."

Marshal Verdugo opens his mouth and closes it again. General Carville looks thoughtful. I don't bother with the others who I don't know, but look up at Lang.

"Do you wish him alive?" Lang asks.

The emperor's eyebrow raises again. "If I decide to treat with him, he must be alive to hear my terms. If I decide to execute him, you have my promise that you may watch."

Lang nods. "Then I will bring him to you."

"If you ally with him against me," the emperor says, "then you will share his fate as I decide it."

"Understood," Lang says.

"Mademoiselle Sturm," the emperor says, and though he has never once raised his voice during the whole interview, my guts clench with anxiety.

"Sir," I say, because it still seems like the safest way to address a military emperor.

"I offer you the same terms," he says. "And the same warning. You have chosen to wear my uniform; if you act against me now, it will be treason."

It is no easy thing to bear the emperor's gaze, and even the dream world doesn't feel like far enough to run from his displeasure. I swallow and nod, unable to form any reply. At least I'm still holding Lang's hand, for otherwise I might do something cowardly, like bolting toward the open windows to fly into the night.

"I will enter the city at dawn," the emperor says to us. "You are dismissed." To his officers, he adds, "Do not hinder them."

I look at Lang, and he nods to the tall glass doors that stand open at the side of the ballroom. We take a few steps in that direction before the emperor speaks again. "Your map, mademoiselle."

We stop. Will he give it to us? But no, he holds nothing out, nor signals his soldiers to do so. He stands with his hands clasped behind him and a mocking curl to his lip.

"So far, it shows us that the king remains within his palace," he says. "I understand there are at least two hundred public rooms." Again the arch of the imperial eyebrow. "Good luck."

"We will find him," Lang says, his voice strong and confident. He tugs my hand, and we walk out the doors to the balcony.

CHAPTER TWENTY-THREE

I HALF expect to find a guard on the balcony, but it's empty. When we reach the railing, I see why. We're high up on a second or third floor. A wide reflecting pool below separates this mansion from a garden which is filled with soldiers' tents. Anyone coming this way would have to pass the troops and wade through the water, avoiding the swans which swim agitatedly below, before they had a chance to scale the wall. It won't be hard, though, to come and go on the wing.

"So we must search the palace?" I ask. "And find the king before the emperor's men do?" If someone else brings King Karl to the emperor before Lang does, then Lang will still be labeled a traitor to the empire. There's more than Lang's revenge at stake now.

Lang nods, but he isn't looking at me. Instead, his eyes scan the gardens, where the dark night is punched through with small fires the soldiers have made after pulling down the ornamental hedges. Then he turns and looks at the building behind us, a tall, pale yellow edifice lit gold with the firelight.

"We're still on the eastern side of the river," he says. "This is a summer residence, not far from the capital. The emperor must plan to ride triumphant into the city in the morning."

A figure approaches from inside the ballroom, silhouetted briefly against the lamplight. Ensign Keller steps out beside us.

"You made me a promise," he says.

"I haven't forgotten it," I reply.

"What promise?" Lang asks. He looks appraisingly at the ensign. "Keller, isn't it?"

I'm surprised Lang knows him, then I remember they were in the same regiment under General Carville until Lang was traded away for Marshal Verdugo. There's every chance that Keller knows my brother too, but I don't dare ask him if he has any news of Fritz.

Keller nods and swallows. He's still clutching his notebook, and I see the whites of his eyes as he looks between me and Lang.

"He helped me while I was searching for you," I say. "I promised I would speak to you on his behalf."

"Then I will listen," Lang says.

I pull him further from the open doors to the ballroom, away from the ears of the men inside, who surely haven't forgotten us. Keller trails after us. "You were born in a body not your own," I say softly to Lang. "And you had to learn a way to make your body as you were meant to be. You found the way to change others, as well, for you changed me and you changed Godfather Drosselmeier. Couldn't you do the same for Keller?"

Lang looks at me, then at the ensign, who is looking down at his notebook and biting his lip.

"What transformation do you seek?" he asks.

"I wish to have a man's body," Keller whispers.

Lang looks at him, really looks, and I feel the moment when he sees beyond the simple expectation of who's allowed to serve the army in an ensign's uniform. "Ah," he says. "Yes. Yes, I can do this for you. But I can't do it now."

The ensign, who had turned his face up hopefully, looks down again.

"I must reserve my strength for what lies ahead," Lang says. He tilts his head, considering. "You helped Mademoiselle Sturm before. Come with us, help us on our way to the palace, and I swear I will do as you ask when Karl is given over to the emperor."

Ensign Keller hesitates, but only for a moment. Then he says, "I'll find horses for you."

He leads us back into the ballroom, through a side door, and down an innumerable number of stairs until we reach the outside of the summer residence and the place where a group of horses is picketed. Keller points out the mounts captured during the day's action, and Lang chooses two for us while the ensign saddles his own white stallion.

We ride into the night. No one questions a trio of hussars who must be on the emperor's business, and soon our horses rumble across one of the wooden pontoon bridges and we enter the king's city.

The streets are full of soldiers, mounted or marching. Some of the houses are shut tight, with their windows shuttered. Others have their doors broken in. On one street we pass a fire, where I finally see some of the townspeople working with the soldiers to pass buckets and douse the flames. If the city burns, it will be no use to either king or emperor. When I look up at the sky, I see orange light reflected in the clouds and know this must not be the only fire.

Then we come to the palace grounds, and I forget about the danger to the city. There's a wide parade ground, full of troops of all sorts. On the far side is the palace, so big that it might be a walled city on its own. Bonfires on the parade ground and torches on the walls light it up with dancing orange light, so it seems like the palace might also catch flame at any moment.

The summer residence was larger than any house in my city, larger than the count's castle I visited once when my father had business there. This palace is larger still. In the dark and confusion of light from the fires, I can't tell where its walls end and the night begins.

Keller is looking at it with the same awe. "How will you find the king?" he asks.

"I was born in this palace," Lang replies. "I spent many years between its walls. I know where to seek him."

We add the horses to one of the pickets, then Lang leads us to the edge of the parade ground, right up to the smooth wall of the palace. Except it isn't so smooth: his fingers find a hidden latch, and he opens a narrow door within the wall. I follow him through while Keller hesitates on the threshold.

"You could stay with the horses," Lang says. "But I don't know that we will return this same way."

Keller sets his jaw. "I'm coming with you," he says, and ducks into the passageway.

Lang lets the door swing shut. There's a click, and for a moment we're enclosed in musty darkness. I freeze, telling myself that Lang wouldn't bring us into a trap, that my eyes will adjust to the dark, that there wouldn't be a door if it didn't lead to somewhere. Then there's a rustle and a spark, and Keller lights a stub of candle he must have had in his sabretache. The little light dances on stone walls thick with accumulated spider webs and dusty grime.

"Don't touch anything," Lang says. "Let's not leave more signs of our passage than we have to."

Keller nods. I take Lang's hand, then hold my other hand out to the ensign. If we move abruptly into the dream world, I can't in good conscience leave him behind.

He looks at me strangely, then reluctantly puts his hand in mine. Despite the close atmosphere of the passage, his skin is cold and clammy, and I can't blame him. What with encountering the emperor and anticipating finding the king ahead, I feel woozy with anxiety myself.

Lang leads us through the passageway. It's narrow enough that we must go single file. Little of the light from Keller's candle reaches him, but Lang never hesitates, even when the first passage meets with others that split off into a dark maze. And why would he hesitate? He spoke truly when he told Keller the time he spent between these walls.

We pass from the outer shell of the palace to the interior. Now there are occasional pinpricks of light where peepholes provide a glimpse into rooms, but still the narrow passages continue. Is the entire palace a warren of secret tunnels?

Lang pauses occasionally to look through the peepholes, and Keller and I look too. Rooms with marble or parquet floors, fresco-painted ceilings, delicate furniture covered in gold leaf and upholstered in bright silks, heavy portraits hanging from walls decorated with motifs of flowers or birds. Some rooms are empty, with the beautiful furniture smashed. Some are as yet untouched. Some have groups of soldiers in them. Then we pass a room where a female voice is screaming and sobbing, and Lang won't let us look, only hurries us along.

Keller's candle burns out, and he grips my hand more tightly in the dusty darkness. We've been moving quietly through the walls for so long, I think that dawn must be breaking over the ruined city soon. I think of Lang's mother, banished to this strange space within the palace, yet separated from all the luxuries that it holds. I even begin to think of these tunnels as a separate realm, like the dream world or the high forest where the mother of the winds lives.

And then, when I start to worry that I'll be trapped in this narrow twisting dark forever and never spread my wings in the open sky again, Lang halts and puts his lips to my ear. "We'll go in here."

CHAPTER TWENTY-FOUR

LANG undoes a latch, and we step through an opening in the wall paneling. At first, I think we've come outside again. The warm, thick air smells of smoke, and I see a glint of stars above us. Then I realize the stars are picked out in gold on a high ceiling painted deep blue. There is an odd tinge to the smoky smell: something herbal that I can't identify.

"What is this place?" Keller whispers.

I look around at the room, which bears little resemblance to the sumptuous chambers we glimpsed in other parts of the palace. Instead of chandeliers, there are hanging lanterns embedded with multicolored glass that give a peculiar glow to shelves piled with books and birds' nests, glass globes and astrolabes, dried flowers and smooth, colored stones. A wide worktable covered with piled papers and bottles in blue and green and yellow stands on one side of the room, while on the other a few heavy chairs face a dark fireplace.

"The royal astrologer's library," Lang says. "Now the domain of Princess Paula Maria." He raises his voice. "Isn't that right, cousin?"

A woman rises from one of the chairs facing the fireplace and turns to look at us. She wears a modified version of the white military jacket that Lang wore when I found him at the head of von Kamptz's army, but over a blood-red skirt, rather than breeches. The colored light of the lanterns plays strangely over her features, but I can see her wry smile, unsettlingly familiar to the one Lang has so often given me.

"Welcome home, dearest Dietrich," she says. Her voice is warm and perfectly modulated, but the words ring hollow to my ear. "Who are your companions?"

"They are not your concern," he replies. "Where are my rings?"

Her face shifts to a delicate frown. Keller tugs my hand and mouths *Rings?* at me, but I shake my head. This isn't the time or the place to explain about Lang's rings. I have no idea how the princess will react to Lang's presence or his questions. I need to keep my attention on her, in case I have to take us quickly into the dream.

"What are you speaking of?" she asks, her tone still the exactly polite diction one would expect from royalty.

"My rings," Lang repeats. "You took them from me. I will have them back now, if you please."

Her frown deepens. When she speaks again, the syrupy tone is gone. "You've broken the enchantment," she says flatly.

"Yes, dearest cousin," he says, putting a mocking emphasis on the endearment. "I have."

She sighs and smooths her hands over her skirts. "I told Father it wouldn't hold."

"And where is my illustrious uncle?" Lang asks.

The princess doesn't answer, only frowns again. "I did think it would last longer than this," she mutters. "Where did I go wrong?" She brushes past us to the worktable and runs her finger along the page of an open book that lies there.

Keller shifts nervously and pulls out of my grasp, backing towards the hidden door we entered through. I let him go. I don't blame him for being nervous about magic, for all that he hopes it will be an answer to his predicament. The princess doesn't seem to be a threat to him, though, nor is she leaping forward with any new spell to stop Lang.

I release Lang as well, so he'll have both hands free, but I stay close to him. I don't know what the princess intends with the book, and it's a relief when Lang steps up to the table and flips it shut on her searching finger.

She makes an indignant noise and looks angrily up at him.

"Where is your father?" Lang asks.

The princess pulls her hand from between the pages of the heavy book. "He's gone," she says shortly.

"But not far," Lang replies. "Which bolt-hole is he hiding in?"

"Why should I tell you?" she asks. "You'll kill him, and then what will become of me?" She reaches for the book again, but Lang pushes it out of her reach.

"I won't kill him," he says. "The emperor will be here at dawn. He wishes to speak to the king."

"The emperor?" the princess says in surprise. Then her face clears and she says, "I should have gone with Mother, but she wouldn't wait for me to bring the books. I can't let anyone else pack them."

She trails off and makes a sudden grab for the book. Lang is quicker, though, and he knocks the book to the floor. It lands with a heavy smack. A little cloud of dust puffs up from the faded carpet. When she starts after it, he sets his foot on it so she can't pick it up.

"Ensign Keller," Lang says, not looking away from his cousin, who is giving him an absolutely furious look. "Light a fire."

It's a sweltering summer night, and this room is warm enough that I already have a line of sweat trickling down my back. Keller, though, is used to taking orders. He goes to the fireplace and takes out his flint.

"Stop," the princess says.

Keller glances at Lang, and continues, sending a few sparks into the dry kindling laid in the fireplace.

"I order you to stop at once!" she says.

Her voice becomes so imperious that Keller pauses, but only briefly. She may be a princess, but she's a von Kamptz princess, and he follows the emperor's cause. He strikes again, and a tiny flame blooms on the hearth.

The princess whirls back to Lang. "Don't burn the books," she says.

"No one should have the knowledge that they contain," he replies.

"No one but you, you mean," she says.

"I learned what I needed to survive," Lang says. He scoops the book from the floor and tosses it to Keller. "No one should be able to do what was done to us."

"Truly, you should have been my father's heir," she spits back. "You are every bit as self-serving as he is."

I grab Lang's arm before he can move toward her. "She's baiting you," I say.

He subsides a little, but I can feel the tense anger in his body. Then he takes a deep breath. "I want nothing of your father's," he says. "Karl has done many evil things, and so did my mother in her turn, but we don't have to continue what they started. It can end. We can end it."

Paula Maria stares at him, her face flat.

"Think of it," I say. "No more curses."

"Who are you?" the princess asks, turning on me.

"I am the clockmaker's goddaughter," I say. "He told me your story, Princess Pirlipat."

"Don't call me that," she snaps.

"He told me how you were cursed and how your curse was broken," I say. "I know the clockmaker's nephew saved you."

"The clockmaker's nephew?" she asks. Her face goes soft and wondering for a moment, but only a moment. She has the same trick that Lang does, of closing off her emotions from her outward appearance. I saw that brief flash, though, and it tells me where to push.

"I've met him," I say. I let go of Lang's arm and step toward her. "I know where he is. I could take you to him."

"But he is cursed," she says softly. "As I was. As we were."

"I broke his curse," I tell her. "And now he's a prince in a kingdom of his own, far away from here. Far away from this war."

She blinks at me, the only sign of discomposure on her face, which she holds in a soft, half-smile that seems to invite confidences. She might be one of the doll companions the nutcracker fashioned in her absence. She blinks again and says, "If you broke his curse, then why are you not with him?"

"Because he was meant to be your cavalier, not mine," I say.

I try to remember the story as Godfather told it to me. Lang's mother cursed the princess, transforming her into a hideous wooden doll. Young Drosselmeier nearly succeeded in breaking the curse, but accidentally took it on himself instead.

The princess had looked favorably on young Drosselmeier until she saw how he had been changed. Then she had been frightened, and why not? To be faced with the same monster she'd seen in the mirror for so many years, just when she thought she was free of the curse—it must have been terrifying. But Drosselmeier isn't trapped in the nutcracker doll's body any longer.

"He waits for you," I say. I hold my hand out to her, but she turns and moves away. Though her back is to us, I see her shoulders hunch as she brings her hands up to cover her face.

"What are you doing?" Lang whispers into my ear. Now he's the one setting a hand on my arm to pull me back. "She's dangerous."

"You said magic broke everything," I whisper back. "This is a chance for magic to fix things."

"By taking her into the dream?" he asks. "You don't know what her mind will do to that realm. You don't know what will happen when she meets the nutcracker and sees that he's broken too."

"You saw the doll-princesses he keeps with him," I say. "Did you see her face when I started speaking of him?" I take his hand in mine. "They need each other. Maybe they won't like what they find in each other, but they at least deserve the chance to try."

He's still frowning, so I add, "Besides, it will give you the opportunity to search this place without her."

Now his eyes widen, and his hand tightens on mine. "We can't separate," he says. "I won't lose you again."

"I'll be back before you know it," I say. "I promise." I press a kiss to his lips, tug out of his grasp, and go to the princess.

She drops her hands as I approach, composing her face over whatever emotions she had to turn away to conceal.

"Will you come with me?" I ask her.

She blinks, then nods minutely and takes my outstretched hand.

Chapter Twenty-Five

I TAKE the princess to the orangery. It's night in the dream world, for it always seems to be the same time as the waking world when I arrive. The air is fresh and cool and sweet after the hot smokiness of the von Kamptz palace and the astrologer's library, and at first that's all I can perceive. The orangery has no chandeliers lit, no candles or lanterns or torches to cast light through the confusion of potted trees.

I could make a lantern appear, but I hesitate to act so blatantly in front of the princess, or in this part of the dream realm which I think of as the nutcracker's.

"This way, Princess," I say, and lead her through the shadowy shapes of the fruit trees. My eyes are adjusting. There's a faint glimmer through the glass panes that make up the ceiling and walls of the orangery. Dawn is coming.

"What is this place?" she whispers as we come to the door. "I know this place."

I open the doors, and golden light spills over us from candles set in sconces along the walls. They illuminate a wide gallery. The walls are made of panels of hard candy, alternating in color between cherry red and lemon yellow. At regular intervals, alcoves hold statues carved from white sugar loaves.

"I know this place," the princess repeats, her voice dazed. She lets go of my hand, takes a few steps into the gallery, and turns about, looking at the statues. Her pale face is lit gold by the candlelight, and her blond hair seems to glitter like the sugar around her.

"This is young Drosselmeier's castle," I say.

The bewildered amazement on her face turns into something sharp and indignant. "It is *my* castle," she says—and, of course, it must be. She was cursed before he was.

"Then he has kept it in your absence, Your Highness," I say carefully. Where is he, anyway? Perhaps I guessed wrong and we won't find him here. He might be in the waking world now—but my instinct says he'll be here, in these sugared halls.

Princess Paula Maria turns on her heel and strides purposefully through the gallery. I trot after her. She's a little shorter than I am, but she moves quickly. We reach the doors I know open to a hall of crystal and gold furnishings before she stops and faces me.

"How did you come here?" she asks. "How did you bring me?"

"Young Drosselmeier brought me here when I was a child," I tell her. "Later I learned the trick of coming and going."

"How?" she asks. "Was it in one of the books Dietrich destroyed?"

I shake my head as she mutters something else under her breath. I'm tempted to defend Lang's actions, but I'm not sure that I disagree with her on this point. The idea of destroying books hurts—and he's likely tossing the astrologer's books into the fire right now. Still, the knowledge in those books has been used to hurt so many people. Maybe it's better to have it remain unknown. In any case, I have to find Drosselmeier and return to the waking world.

"Young Drosselmeier showed me the way once," I say. "I wanted to return to this realm, and I waited for him to take me again. But then one day I realized that if he could travel back and forth, there had to be a way for me to do it as well. There was no book, and nothing written down. I only wanted it very badly."

She stares at me. "You…" she says. "You *wanted it very badly*, and the way was shown to you? I've wished for years just to know if this place still existed, or if it winked out of being in the moment that the curse was broken."

"But the curse wasn't broken," I tell her. "Only transferred to him."

"And he was trapped, as I was," she says softly. She's crying, I realize. There are tears streaking down through the powder on her face.

"His curse is broken now. Or half broken," I amend. "It wasn't as strong as when it bound you. But—" I stop, for how much can I tell her? The curse might be half broken, but so is the nutcracker. "I think he needs you," I say. "To unravel what remains of the spell."

She nods, still weeping silently. I wait until she gathers herself and delicately wipes at her eyes with the backs of her thumbs. "I know what my father did," she says. "Perhaps Dietrich is right to want to kill him, when we've all suffered so much because of his actions."

"Dietrich will bring the king to the emperor," I say. "He gave his word to do so, and to let the emperor stand judgment on him."

"Then perhaps he will," she says, though her tone doesn't imply any great confidence in Lang keeping that promise.

I can imagine the Lang I met last winter giving his word to the emperor with no particular intention of following through. He would never have given up the idea of killing his uncle himself, or admitted that his mother was partly to blame for the tangled weave of curses and pain that trapped him along with his cousin and the nutcracker. The Lang of a year ago had no thought beyond exacting revenge on everyone who'd hurt him and his family, but he's not the same man now. Now he has me, and an inkling of what life might be when these battles are over.

The princess pushes open the doors at the end of the gallery. A cascade of glittering light pours out, and I'm temporarily blinded by its brightness after the low light of the gallery. The crystal hall is filled with candles, and the light reflects off the walls, bouncing and multiplying until the space is as bright as midday.

As my vision recovers, the first thing I see are the doll-princesses. They sit in a cluster near a chaise lounge. Young Drosselmeier is at the center, sitting up. He must have been sleeping, but now he blinks at us.

The real Paula Maria walks to him. He stands, his eyes still wide, and his mouth hanging open as he looks at her. When she's two paces away, he goes down on one knee and holds his hands out to her. "My lady," he says.

She moves forward and clasps his fingers in hers. "Rise," she says. "You have done me a great service and paid a heavy price. It is I who ought to kneel to you, for I am forever in your debt."

He comes slowly to his feet, trembling before her. One by one, the doll-princesses disappear, and it is only the two of them standing together in the center of the light-filled crystal hall.

"You may leave us," the princess says. She doesn't look away from young Drosselmeier, but the words are clearly for me, and just as clearly a command.

It's a command I don't mind following, for I'm eager to return to Lang. Before I can go, however, there is one more matter to address.

"Where are the rings?" I ask. "The ones you took from Dietrich?"

Now she does look at me, her eyes narrowed in annoyance. Young Drosselmeier, too, glances at me in puzzlement. He doesn't even recognize me, I think: the appearance of the true princess has erased me from his memory as surely as it disappeared the doll-princesses. Even so, his gaze is more clear-eyed and perceptive than I've ever seen it before.

The princess sighs and nods her head gracefully, as if she's decided to grant me a royal favor. "You have helped me," she admits, "so I suppose I'll tell you."

"Thank you, Your Highness," I say.

"I returned them to those who bore them first," she says. "And I made sure that they were laid to rest in the crypt, for they were a part of the royal line." She pauses and tilts her head, considering briefly before she adds, "You'll find my father there as well. He fled into the crypt. There are tunnels. Dietrich will know."

"Thank you," I say again. I retreat slowly toward the door, not wanting to turn my back and offend her at the last moment.

As I reach the doorway, she says, "You may tell Dietrich that I bear him no ill will. All is finished between us."

"I will," I promise, and step out of the hall. The princess and the nutcracker turn back to each other. I close the doors.

Somewhere in the castle bells chime, and I hear a patter of footsteps, overlaid with chattering voices. There's sunlight flowing through the windows of the gallery now, overwhelming the glow of the candles. Dawn has come, though I don't think it was more than a few minutes that I stood within the crystal hall.

A group of brilliantly dressed courtiers enter the gallery and look at me curiously. Then a page comes from another entrance, carrying a tray with steaming cups of coffee and hot chocolate. The bells are still ringing, and all around me is the sense that the castle is coming to life and filling up with people. Paula Maria's idea of the dreamworld is overlaying and reinforcing that of young Drosselmeier's.

I step out of the way of the page with his heavy tray, and return to the orangery. Now that it's light, it takes only a moment to find the saber Lang dropped on the stone tiles after I put the ring on his finger. I pick it up and yawn, returning myself to the waking world.

Chapter Twenty-Six

In the astrologer's library, only a few moments have passed since I left with the princess. Lang stands by the table and Keller is still kneeling at the fireplace, though his tiny flame has gone out while he stares at me.

"What happened to the princess?" the ensign asks, as I set the saber down on the cluttered table.

Lang doesn't say anything, just moves quickly to fold me into his arms.

"I don't think my heart beat a single time while you were gone," he says softly into my hair.

"Then it's good that I wasn't gone long," I say. I hug him back, tucking myself against his chest. There's the familiar ache of weariness in my bones after the double transfer between worlds, but it's not so much that I'm worried.

He takes a deep breath and rests his forehead against my temple. "Always killing adders," he says.

"I can't help it," I reply.

"Next time, take me with you," he says.

"I will," I promise, but I don't think there will be a next time. I shift to take his hand in mine, and feel the ring on his finger. It reminds me of our purpose here. "I brought the princess to young Drosselmeier," I say. "And she told me where your rings and her father are."

"Where?" Lang asks immediately.

Keller says, "Who is Drosselmeier?" I don't think he's expecting an answer at this point, though, for he continues muttering to himself in low tones.

"In the crypt," I tell Lang. I squeeze his hand, knowing the next words won't be easy ones for him to hear. "She said she returned the rings to your brothers." I feel his indrawn breath and see the lines deepen around his mouth. "And that the king had fled there—she said you'd know the tunnels."

"Then we'll go to the crypt," he says.

"And the fire?" Keller asks. "Am I still building a fire?"

His words finally penetrate to Lang, who looks at him. "Forget the fire for now, ensign. This is more important."

"Yes, sir," Keller says, though the words carry more than a hint of exasperation. He stands and brushes soot from the knees of his pants.

"Are you still coming with us?" I ask. Maybe a visit to the royal crypts is more than the ensign has bargained for.

He looks at me, and then at Lang. "Are your lives always like this?" he asks. "Curses? And dreams? And whatever you did with the princess? What will the emperor say when he finds his prospective bride has vanished? What will happen once your magic touches me?" He frowns. "Maybe it's already too late. I'm already mixed up in this. How can I go back to General Carville?

He'll discharge me now for sure, and then where will I go? I can't go home."

"Ensign!" Lang says sharply, cutting into Keller's anxious monologue.

Keller stops talking and looks at him.

"You can always tell the general that you followed us to gather information," Lang says. "Or even that you were coerced to help us. And," he adds, "I will do no magic to you that you don't wish for. Too much has been done to me without asking. I won't do the same to anyone else." He places his hand over his heart. "I swear it on my mother's memory."

Keller still doesn't have answers to any of his questions, and I doubt he knows what happened to Lang's mother, but he hears the sincerity in Lang's voice. Slowly, he nods.

"Very well," he says. "To the crypts, then?"

"Yes," Lang says. He picks up the saber by its gold-chased hilt and looks at the naked blade. "Is this from the dream?" he asks me.

"It is the sword of a von Kamptz prince," I say. "You dropped it in the orangery when I recalled you to yourself."

He steps away from me and swings it a few times, testing the weight and balance of it. "I will carry it," he says. "For now."

We go through the hidden passageways again, but not so far this time. Lang brings us out into a corridor lined with gleaming marble stone as red as blood. A high window reflects darkness back at us. It's still night here in the waking world.

How much longer till dawn breaks here? When will the emperor arrive to judge King Karl—and us?

"Do you have a pocket watch?" I ask Keller, but he only

shakes his head.

We walk down the corridor away from the window. It ends at a pair of heavy doors made of dark wood and covered with thick plates of silver embossed with the von Kamptz crest. When Lang pushes and tugs at the doors, nothing happens.

"Locked," he growls, though that doesn't stop him from pulling at the handle again.

"Can't you magic them open?" Keller asks.

"No." Lang begins pacing back and forth across the width of the corridor. He twitches the naked saber in the air like the tail of an angry cat.

There's a small space under the doors, enough for a whiff of cool, musty air to escape from what lies beyond. Lang could make himself a mouse and slip beneath, but then he'd have to change again to open it from the inside. He needs to save his energy for the confrontation with his uncle.

I reach to twist the ring around my finger, remember that Lang has it, and curl my finger into the gold chain that hangs about my neck instead. Tugging it shifts the little golden key that hangs between my breasts beneath my clothing. Of course—the key.

"I might be able to open the door," I say.

I draw the key out and go to the massive doors. Even the lock is huge, big enough that I could stick my whole finger into it. The tumblers inside must be equally large and heavy, and the key to move them must be as big as my whole hand.

The golden key I have is tiny, but I unthread it from the chain and hold it up. Keller looks at me and raises an eyebrow, but he's given up on questions for now. Lang is still pacing restlessly, though I'm sure he's keeping an eye on me as well.

If the von Kamptzes are so accustomed to magic, there's every chance that this lock could be enchanted too. I have to try, though. If we can't catch King Karl, Lang will never rest. Neither do I relish the thought of disappointing the emperor.

I take the golden key and insert it into the large open space of the lock. It's so obviously the wrong key for the door. I can feel Keller's puzzled gaze on me, but the ghost's repeated whine rings in my ears. *Keys open locks. Keys open doors.*

I turn the key, and though it touches nothing in the oversized keyhole, I feel resistance, as if it pushes against the very air. I clasp my hands together around the tiny key and turn it again.

This time there's a grinding noise, followed by a series of thunks. Then the resistance is gone so suddenly that the golden key spins out of my hand. It hits the marble floor, bounces once, and slides underneath the door while I swear.

Lang comes back to stand next to me. "Did it work?" he asks.

"I hope so," I say. "I went through a lot of trouble to keep that key for myself. If the doors won't open and I can't get it back, I'm going to be upset."

Lang squares his shoulders and pulls at the doors again.

They swing open, smoothly and silently, revealing a yawning blackness punctuated by a few torches. It's a stairway made of the same red marble, dropping away into the dark. It's not particularly inviting, but I wouldn't expect the entrance to a crypt to be a welcoming sight.

Lang stoops, picks up the golden key, and hands it to me. I put it safely back onto the chain. As I'm reattaching the clasp at the nape of my neck, there's a sudden rumble of voices and footsteps behind us.

I turn to see a group of soldiers coming down the hall. Part of the Grand Army, for they aren't wearing the von Kamptz red and white. I'd managed to forget that the emperor was sending other men in search of King Karl, but I remember it now. I step toward the doorway, and Lang moves between me and the oncoming men.

"Lang?" one of them calls, and my knees go weak with relief. It's my brother, Fritz.

Lang lowers his sword as the soldiers come up to us: my brother, Ernst Hatt, and another hussar whose name I can't remember. There are also two infantrymen who I've never seen before, but I'm glad they're on our side, for they carry long rifles and could have shot us from the other end of the hall.

Fritz has a captain's third stripe on his cuffs now. It must be a recent promotion, for he didn't mention it in the last letters we received at home. He steps ahead of the others, staring at us. "What are you doing here?"

I open my mouth to attempt an explanation, and perhaps Keller does the same, for Fritz makes an impatient motion with his hand. "Not you, ensign. Lang."

I'm indignant for a brief moment. Now even my brother doesn't recognize me? Then I remember I don't want to be recognized among the soldiers, that I cut my hair and put on my brother's old uniform to prevent being seen immediately for a woman. Of course my brother knows me. He's just quick-thinking enough not to give me away.

"We're going to capture a king," Lang says. "Would you care to come along?"

Chapter Twenty-Seven

FRITZ and his companions stare at Lang.

"Karl has gone to ground," Lang says impatiently. "Either you come along with us, or you may keep searching on your own."

"But—" says the cavalryman whose name I can't recall. "You were—"

"If he brings King Karl to the emperor, then he's forgiven," Ensign Keller puts in.

Lang nods. "I am following the direction of the emperor."

My brother looks at me and raises one eyebrow, ever so slightly. *True?*

I nod. *Yes.*

I see his mouth tighten. *Very well.*

"We go where Lang goes," he says to his men. "If he's telling the truth, we capture the traitorous king. If he's lying, we capture the traitorous prince. In either case, we serve the interests of the emperor."

Lang and Fritz look at each other for a long moment. Then

Lang says, "That's as fair as I can hope for." He nods to the marble staircase. "But there are still other ways out. Let's not give Karl any more time to reach them."

We all step through the massive doorway, and Lang pushes the doors closed. On this side, there's a mechanism to close the lock again, which he turns. It engages with a satisfyingly heavy click. We all look around at our companions, then Ernst and Keller take the two closest torches from the wall sconces, and we start down the stairs.

Fritz catches me by the arm, and we let the others go down the slick marble steps.

"Are you—" he starts to ask me, but doesn't finish the question. Probably because it's not just one, but several dozen questions, and how can he choose which to ask first?

"I'm glad to see you alive and in one piece," I tell him. "And I'm glad to be alive myself."

I begin moving down the steps again, not wanting to lose sight of Lang as the stairwell curves down into darkness. "I got your message," I tell my brother as he keeps pace beside me. "And I found Lang." I reach out to squeeze his hand briefly, then tug at his cuff. "Thank you, Captain Stahlbaum."

He glances at the triple line of braid on the end of his sleeve and brushes away an imperceptible bit of something. "It seemed like the right thing to do," he says. It's the closest to approval he's ever gotten when speaking about my connection with Lang. "And now the king?" he asks.

"We met with the emperor, and he personally asked us to bring King Karl to him," I say. Seeing the way my brother's eyebrows go up at that is quite satisfying, even with the memory of the emperor's overwhelming presence fresh in my mind. "It's a long story, though."

Fritz looks appraisingly at me, then shakes his head. "I look forward to hearing it," he says. He points down the stairs, where the others have all paused at a sign from Lang. He watches Fritz and me approach. Only when his eyes meet mine does he start forward again.

The stairwell continues down and down, and my thoughts descend into dark places along with my feet. When I was searching for my niece Clara, I climbed an endless set of stairs in a tower in the nutcracker's marzipan castle. That time I went up alone, and a monster surprised us at the top. This time I'm going down as part of a group, and it's the monster we're hoping to surprise.

Everyone is concentrating on their footing. The soldiers don't speak, and there's nothing to hear but our own breathing. The sound echoes back at us in eerie wheezes, punctuated by the tread of boots on stone.

I should be thinking about what the crypt will be like, what the king might do when we find him, or how our next conversation with the emperor will go. Instead, my mind fixes on the fact that every step down takes us further from the open air and the sky.

Whatever we discover at the bottom of these stairs, I won't be able to fly away from it, and I'm even more wary of returning to the dream world now that Princess Paula Maria and young Drosselmeier are united there. I don't trust that either of them will want to help Lang and me. The dream world is not without its dangers, and even if I have some control over what happens there, I am only one imagination and now they are two together.

All these thoughts bring me back to the conclusion that

what waits beneath the palace must be faced head on. I'm glad that Fritz and his party came upon us, so we're eight now against whoever guards King Karl.

We turn another curve, and there, finally, is the end of the descent. The red marble that covered the stairs ends, and the passageway that stretches before us is hewn from dark rock.

The walls are only intermittently visible, though. This underground space isn't merely a crypt. It's an ossuary, with bones stacked along the walls in repeating patterns. These are not like the dead who lay abandoned on the battlefield where they fell, but bodies which have been carefully disassembled and rearranged as decoration.

More than one of the men makes a sign against evil, and we all draw closer together. Lang still holds his prince's saber in his right hand, but with his left, he waves us forward before taking my hand.

"Who are they?" I whisper to him.

"This has been the seat of von Kamptz power for hundreds of years," he says. "Many have had the chance to die in service to the royal family."

That is slightly more comforting than thinking these innumerable bones are the result of something like the battlefields I've seen, but I'd still rather be in the open air with the sky above me.

Even the ceiling has been covered in weathered ivory pieces, as if we've walked into the very belly of death. It is all strange and terrible, and yet somehow beautiful as well. I think again of the jumbled bodies on the battlefield, whose deaths are a monument to disorder. In the ossuary, at least there's the sense that these bones have been cared for, with each set in its particular place.

The first chamber is followed by a narrower corridor lined with small rooms. The side rooms are still decorated with bones, but carved marble sarcophagi rest on platforms in the center of each. In the flickering torchlight, I catch glimpses of stone faces wearing crowns and holding swords.

We pass half a dozen chambers before something inside one catches Lang's attention. His face goes absolutely blank as he turns to address the rest of the group.

"Wait here," he says. "Keep watch." To me, he adds, "Stay close to Captain Stahlbaum."

Ernst hands him a torch, and he steps into the small space. There is no ornate marble coffin. Instead, the flame lights a line of shrouded bodies on the central platform, each one smaller than the next. Time has shrunken the remains, but the last of Lang's brothers can't have been more than two or three years old when he was killed.

My stomach sickens at the thought. I already knew they were only children, but to see these tiny bundles of bones before me—when Fritz whispers a question in my ear, it takes several deep breaths before I can reply. "His brothers."

Fritz takes this information and redirects the other soldiers, who've been peering curiously into the tomb, to move to positions a little way up and down the corridor. He stations himself in the doorway, looking outward, and I stand beside him, giving Lang some measure of privacy with the remains of his family.

Seven brothers dead, and the eighth left alone in the world.

I sidestep closer to Fritz and press my shoulder against his. He looks down at me and wrinkles his nose while squinting his eyes, the face he always used to make when we were children and I was crying and he was trying to get me to laugh instead.

When it doesn't work, he leans over and says into my ear, "He has us, and that's not nothing."

I nod and swallow hard against the tightness in my throat. I want to hug Fritz, and I want to drag him with me through the dream world so we can both hug Luise. Has her second child been born yet? I think of the squalling little creature I expect to meet when I see her next, and of the smallest shroud in the tomb at my back.

Fritz leans his shoulder into me again. "Go to him."

I swallow again and turn to the door of the tomb. Lang has set the torch into a sconce on the wall, but at first, I can't find him in the small room. Then I realize he's sitting on the floor with his knees drawn up and his back against the wall, staring at the still shapes on the platform.

I don't say anything. What is there to say? I sit beside him and put my hand on his knee. After a moment, he twines his fingers around mine. His fingers are bare, so I know he's returned the last ring.

I lean my head on his shoulder while he takes long, shaky breaths. He holds tight to my hand, and I grip him back. He needs this time, but all the while I'm also aware of the soldiers standing guard outside this tomb without knowing why we're here, of the king still lying in wait somewhere among the bones, and of the layers of rock and dirt and palace that separate me from the sky.

When Lang pushes to his feet, I'm relieved, then immediately ashamed of my own feelings. How can I be impatient with Lang, when my own brother is just outside, living and breathing and ready to stand with me? I've had years with my siblings, and

Lang has had only the briefest moments with the cold bones of his family.

I turn to him, trying to think of the proper words to comfort him in this place, in this moment. Unfortunately, we don't have time for comfort. There's a clatter and a shout from the corridor. Lang snatches up the saber he'd set on the floor and rushes out of the tomb.

Chapter Twenty-Eight

Four soldiers with heavy broadswords come in a rush from a doorway further down the corridor. They're tall, heavyset men with brass breastplates covering their chests, and they attack with the force of a battering ram. Fritz and the others move to meet them.

Lang raises the saber in his hand. "Stay here," he says fiercely, pushing me behind him.

I stumble backward as he leaps forward. A burst of sound and light breaks through the crypt as one of the infantrymen kneels with his rifle and shoots at the oncoming von Kamptz soldiers. He aims low and true. The bullet takes out the unarmored knee of the soldier in the lead, who roars and stumbles. Keller throws the torch he's been carrying into the face of another.

My blood thunders in my ears, drowning out the clang of steel meeting steel. I want to fly, but I can't—there's nowhere to fly here. On the battlefield I could dive at an attacker, but I can't do that in this low-ceilinged tunnel.

Lang is in the midst of the fray, though. Whether I have wings or hands, I should be with him. I grab a torch from the wall, intending to follow Keller's example and throw it into someone's face.

The skirmish is already ending, however. Only one of the von Kamptz men still stands. The other three are on the floor, as is an infantryman from our side. Fritz and Ernst are engaged together with the last man, and he falls as my eye finds Lang pulling his saber free from the lifeless body of another soldier.

If I had a sword, I could help—but although my time flying means I have the strength to pick up a saber that's half as long as I am tall, that doesn't mean I know what to do with it. All I know how to fight with is my talons.

I set the torch back into its sconce and go to Lang, stepping over fresh pools of blood and resolving that next time there's a threat, I won't hesitate to change.

"Are you unharmed?" he asks. I nod, and he reaches out to cup my cheek in his hand. "I wanted you away from the fight."

"I know," I say. "But you know I'll always follow you, and I always run toward danger."

His hand shifts to my nape, and he leans his forehead against mine. "I know," he says. "I just wish that it wasn't always so dangerous to be beside me."

"There's no place I'd rather be," I say. "And once we turn von Kamptz over to the emperor, I hope your life will be far less dangerous."

"Yes," Lang says. He straightens, his focus returning. "Now that von Kamptz is defeated, we'll finish this business with the emperor, and then we'll go after whatever you want." He gives me a glimpse of his wry smile. "It will be my turn to follow you."

"I want to fly," I say immediately. "I want to go to the mother of the winds."

"Then that's what we'll do," Lang promises. "You have a story for her, and so do I."

We shift apart and look at the others, who are grouped around the fallen infantryman. His body is disfigured by a deep slash from the enemy's broadsword, and his blood makes a dark pool on the weathered ivory floor. I never even exchanged a word with him, and now I won't.

Fritz kneels beside the dead man to close his eyes, and everyone bows their heads.

"You still owe me for all the tobacco you borrowed, Lichtmann," the remaining infantryman says, his voice rough. "Don't think you get out of it this easily." He pauses, clears his throat, and turns away.

There's a moment of silence, then Fritz turns to Lang. "Where is your king?" he asks. "Because right now it looks less like we're capturing von Kamptz and more like you've been leading us into a trap."

I bristle immediately, but bite my tongue. Whatever happens when we find King Karl, we'll need my brother and his men to stand with us. As captain, my brother outranks Lang—"von Kamptz prince" isn't a rank that holds any weight in the emperor's Grand Army, after all. The rest of the soldiers will follow Fritz and his decisions, but not if he undermines his authority by giving in to his sister's pleading on her lover's behalf.

"The fact that we found a rear guard means we're on the right path," Lang says. He points to the opening opposite the doorway from which the attack came. All I can see are shadows and bones, but I trust that Lang knows these tunnels as the princess said he would. "There's a tunnel that leads up to a residence near the river."

"Go look," my brother tells Ernst.

Ernst takes a torch and lights up the stone-hewn space while the others move cautiously behind him. In addition to the ornate stone sarcophagus, there's a wide carving set into the wall. A thicket of spears and swords come together at the center where a man wearing a crown leads one half of the panel's stone soldiers towards the other half.

"The panel slides to the side," Lang says.

Under his direction, Ernst feels along the line between the two clashing forces and then half of the carving rolls smoothly aside, separating the combatants.

Beyond is a tunnel carved from the bedrock. It contains no bones, though there is another lit torch that shows someone has been here recently.

A breath of cool, damp air issues forth from the opening and whispers past my ear. My heart jumps, for the little draft has the feel of the winds' curious attention. If a wind can find its way through this tunnel, then there must be an outlet back to the sky I've been missing since we entered the palace an age ago.

"You'll go first," Fritz says, pointing to Lang and then to the narrow passageway. "I'll follow you." He indicates the others, placing me in the middle of the group, between Ensign Keller and Ernst Hatt, and directing the infantryman to bring up the rear and shoot anyone attempting to follow us.

Lang enters the tunnel, and the rest of us fall into line behind him. The infantryman pulls the stone panel shut behind us, and my guts twist unhappily as that last passage back to the upper world is closed off.

I've had enough of tunnels and passageways. I ache for the sky. It's an almost physical pain beneath my breastbone. I want to spread my arms, spread my wings, and go up—but there's no room for that. I keep bumping my elbows on the damp stone walls. The ceiling is low enough that all the soldiers have taken off their shakos, and Ernst, who is the tallest among us, has to crouch a little to avoid hitting his head.

How did Lang live like this? When he was a mouse, the tunnels and the passageways between the walls must have felt larger, but still—so much close, stale air and darkness. I no longer have any question of why he chose to learn the transformation into a hawk. The opportunity to move through the sky, where there can be no walls, is the furthest thing imaginable from crawling through these places.

Lost in my thoughts, I nearly run into Keller, who turns back to glare at me with his finger over his lips. The others have stopped too, and I realize I can see all of them because we've come to a slightly larger space.

It's the end of the tunnel. Lang points to a latch on a wooden door set into the stone. Then, with silent motions of his hands, he indicates what will happen next when we rush out to overwhelm whoever is on the other side.

I can still feel that tiny breath of wind in the tunnel. I don't dare say anything aloud, but I think, *Pay attention, little breeze, and you'll have a fine tale to take back to your mother.*

Lang readies his saber in one hand. The other he holds up, so everyone can see as he folds down his fingers.

Five. Four. Three. Two. One.

He yanks open the door, and the soldiers tumble out into

the space beyond.

I dash after them, taking in the scene: a kitchen with a handful of von Kamptz's men. They jump up, swiping ineffectually with their eating knives or reaching for the weapons they laid aside.

One man brandishes a chicken leg, then lobs it at us. I duck beneath it and feel the warm drip of grease falling onto my skin as it flies over my head.

Fritz and Lang have their sabers out, but the infantryman dives ahead of them and hooks his shoulder under the edge of the table where the von Kamptz men were sitting. His momentum overturns the heavy slab of wood, knocking over three of the men and catching the legs of one with a sickening crunch.

Lang vaults over the table, catches a stunned guard by the throat, and presses him against the wall. "Where is the king?" he demands.

"A-a-asleep," the man stammers. "Upstairs."

Lang lets him fall and looks around the room. His eyes meet mine, and this time, instead of telling me to run or hide, he points to the stairs.

Fritz is already headed that way and the other men, having made quick work of the von Kamptz soldiers, soon join us.

There are more guards at the top of the stairs, in a hall covered in faded green damask. Again Lang and Fritz and the others with us engage the enemy with their sabers, and I'm left feeling inadequate to help. Then I spot a most welcome sight: a window at the end of the hall.

It's open. I can see the wind moving the curtain beside it.

Finally, we're close enough to the wide freedom of the sky

that I can change my form. Lang and the emperor's men have pushed this group of von Kamptz soldiers partway down the hall and there's a clear space around me. Without further hesitation, I transform.

As soon as I have my hawk's body, the familiar, fierce joy at having wings fills me. I leap into the air, screaming my own battle cry: *kek-kek-kek!*

One of the von Kamptz soldiers looks up at me, and his eyes go wide.

"The hawk!" he cries. "The prince's hawk!"

Half of the soldiers pause to look at me. Fritz and Lang take advantage of their distraction, and two of the von Kamptz men fall beneath their blades.

Kek-kek-kek, I shriek, and King Karl's soldiers turn and flee.

CHAPTER TWENTY-NINE

I FLUTTER down to Lang's hand. There's room enough to fly in the corridor, but I'm not eager to navigate past the lamps and hanging chandeliers as we continue down the hall and up another staircase. More of von Kamptz's men appear and lose their courage at the sight of me.

Earlier, I worried about the soldiers' gossip about me, but now it's working to our advantage. Whatever they know, or think they know, about Lang, the hawk which followed him in battle, and his sudden disappearance from the middle of the army's commanders, it's clear that they consider me to be the very worst type of omen.

At the top of the second set of stairs is another hallway, and there we find King Karl. If he'd been sleeping after his underground escape before, he's quite awake now. He stands in the hall, red-faced and rumpled, bellowing at the last three men who remain with him.

"It's only a bird," he says. "Stand fast."

Lang lifts his hand, launching me into the air and raising his saber. I swoop over the king's head and scream my *kek-kek-kek* at him and his companions before landing on a crystal-studded chandelier. It swings precipitously beneath me, and I watch from above as Lang approaches his uncle.

"Ah, nephew," the king says. "I wondered what became of you." The soldiers beside the king tremble, but they haven't run yet. I spread my wings, ready to drop down on their heads if they move toward Lang.

"Did you really?" Lang asks. He's two swords' length from the king now. "Or did you merely regret the loss of your puppet?"

The king drops any pretense of politeness, and his face becomes a snarl of anger instead. "You miserable whelp," he spits. "I should have broken your neck like your brothers, except that Paula Maria said she could hold you."

"Obviously she was mistaken," Lang says. "But she and I have come to an understanding."

Karl glares suspiciously at him. "Where is she? What have you done with her?"

"The emperor is considering her for a wife," Lang says. "She could bear future emperors for him."

The glare melts away from Karl's face as he considers this: his grandchildren ruling the Grand Empire. Clearly, it would take some of the sting out of his defeat and the capture of his capital by the emperor.

Lang lets the king savor the idea. He gives the older man long enough to imagine the glittering coronation of a future grandson before he says, "But Paula Maria is gone from the palace. She's reunited with the one you first promised her in marriage to. The clockmaker's nephew."

Immediately, Karl's face goes red with anger again. "Drosselmeier?" he asks. "That half-wit doll?"

"With Drosselmeier," Lang confirms.

He is deadly calm before his uncle's rage. How is it that Karl never learned the trick of shuttering his feelings as his nephew and daughter have? Perhaps he's been king for so long that he hasn't needed to hide his thoughts.

"He's no longer a doll," adds Lang. "I can't say if he's still a half-wit. You did promise her to the one who could break her curse, though, just as you promised to keep peace with the emperor. Today is the day I help you make good on your promises, uncle."

He lunges forward, moving so quickly that the men beside the king have no time to react before Lang's blade is at Karl's throat.

"I've promised you to the emperor and his justice," Lang says as his uncle sputters. "But I think he'll understand if I can't bring you back alive."

King Karl's face is nearly purple. I can see veins pulsing beneath his skin, and I wonder if he'll die in a fit of apoplexy before Lang can do anything to him.

"Tell your men to stand down," Lang says quietly.

The king's jaw works several times, but he says, "Lower your weapons." His soldiers step away and are quickly caught up by Fritz and his men, who bind them and push them into one of the rooms along the hallway. In a few minutes, the king is trussed up and lying on the floor.

With all the gilt and golden braid on his uniform, he looks like a very large and very unhappy golden fish. It's hard to believe this is the man who's caused so much unhappiness for so many people, when he looks so ridiculous.

"Captain Stahlbaum," Lang says to my brother. "We need horses. I have an appointment to keep with the emperor."

Fritz sends two of the men to find mounts, then comes to stand with Lang. "Where are we?" he asks.

"Just beyond the city," Lang says. "Upstream from the bridge." His lip curls briefly. "This is a place where royal mistresses can be kept and visited without bringing them into the palace."

He turns back and prods the king with his foot. "You weren't content with trying to end my grandmother's line," he says. "You had to come and defile her home as well."

Karl twitches, but he's regained some composure. "What of the clockmaker?" he asks. "Where is he?"

"Dead," Lang says.

My brother's mouth flattens in a brief grimace at the memory of how Godfather Drosselmeier died, but he says nothing to interrupt this conversation between Lang and his uncle.

"That's no great loss," Karl replies. "But do you know he might have been your father?"

I raise my wings, ready to fly down and stop up whatever awful thing is about to come out of the king's mouth, but Lang puts his hand up to hold me back.

"He wanted your mother," Karl says. "But she didn't favor him, and my father saw no advantage to the match." His eyes glint, and he almost smiles. "It wasn't difficult to convince him to make the traps for the get of his rival."

Very slowly, Lang crouches down until he's on a level with

the king lying on the floor.

"How joyful you were," he says, "to discover me and to put me to use as a prince-commander at the head of your army. But did it never occur to you that you could have had eight more such as I to fight for you?

"My father and all his sons would have been sworn to you against the emperor. My brothers would have married and brought more allies to your side. Your daughter could've had a happy childhood and been well matched with some other royal house. Even the clockmaker's nephew might have taken up a commission in your army, had you not given the orders against my family."

Lang stands and looks down at his uncle, who appears to be too angry to speak. "Once I thought to kill you," he says. "But now I see there's no need. Your only legitimate heir is gone. Your kingdom has fallen to the emperor. He's marching into your capital, even as we speak. Everything you sought to avoid has come to pass, and by your own hand. I'll give you over to the emperor, and for however many days remain in your life, you'll have the knowledge of your own failure as your constant companion."

By now, Karl has stopped struggling. He doesn't try to reply to Lang, but only glares balefully as Fritz and Ernst pick him up and haul him away.

I fly from the chandelier to Lang's hand, then perch on his shoulder as he follows Fritz and Ernst and their stiff and indignant burden.

Outside, dawn paints the sky pale yellow above a small garden of drooping roses, also pale yellow. Maybe, when this is all over, I'll look for fabric in that color and make a dress out of it. After the long hours in the palace and beneath the earth, this wide-open early morning sky is the most beautiful thing I've ever seen.

The soldiers have found horses and a wagon, into which they put the king. He's still quivering with impotent rage, and as the wagon rumbles along, it's hard to tell if the movements of his body are his own struggles or the jouncing from the road.

We proceed up from the river valley and return to the city. Warm golden light flows like honey over fallen stones and blackened timbers. The fires we saw in the night have run their course, and there are whole buildings missing between their fellows. The emperor's soldiers drowse in doorways or patrol the streets in threes and fours while the townspeople have all but disappeared from view.

The king, lying in the wagon, sees none of this, though he must smell the smoke. With so many soldiers moving about, no one takes any notice of our little party, and we come back again to the wide parade ground before the palace without incident. The troops who pitched their tents here the night before are waking, moving sleepily to rebuild their cook fires or stumbling away to relieve themselves in the strips of greenery along the edges of the parade ground.

The wagon must go slowly through the tents and the soldiers, so we're only halfway across the open expanse before the sound of trumpets and hoofbeats rises behind us. All the soldiers run to form lines, making a corridor of men standing at attention before the approaching riders.

Lang sends me into the sky. From above, I watch the emperor approach the palace at the head of a group of riders. His companions are the same generals and marshals we saw at the summer residence last night. They all look tired, which reminds me of my own weariness. But there's a warm current of air rising with the sun, supporting me as I circle above the parade ground, and I'm eager to see what will happen next.

The emperor and his companions ride at a fast walk, quick enough that they thunder across the cobblestones, but not so quick that they appear to be hurrying to the palace. When he reaches Lang, the emperor pulls up his horse and stops.

I spiral down and perch on the edge of the wagon as Lang steps out of the line of men. "I've brought Karl to you, as you asked," he says, pitching his voice to carry. The soldiers closest to us don't speak or break formation in front of the emperor, but I see them exchange sidelong looks with their fellows.

The emperor tilts his head, ever so slightly, to one side. "Have you?" he asks mildly. He urges his horse forward a few steps and glances into the wagon.

Karl Albert, the last of the von Kamptz kings, spits contemptuously in the emperor's general direction.

"So you have," the emperor says with a thoughtful nod. He waves his hand. "Bring him along, then."

Chapter Thirty

The emperor twitches his reins and continues across the parade ground. His retinue follows at a respectful distance. Lang and our party take a position behind them. From my place on Lang's shoulder, I look around at the soldiers of the emperor's Grand Army. This is the first time I've seen them gathered at attention in daylight hours rather than as dim shapes in the night or flashing uniforms on the battlefield.

They're as diverse as the winds. A few are very pale, and a few very dark, with every shade of weather-beaten, weary face in between. I wonder where their homes are, and if they will settle here or follow the emperor on to his next target.

At the palace, the emperor doesn't pause. He continues on horseback up the wide steps to the grand entrance, the stallion's hooves clattering on the marble.

That is his imperial privilege, apparently, for the others dismount and walk more slowly after him. The wagon we'd commandeered is left behind. Fritz and Ernst hoist Karl up, dragging him along with his head between them. He'll have to close his eyes if he wants to avoid the view of the horse and rider entering his palace.

The air inside is oppressively warm after the cool morning freshness outdoors. No one speaks, but the iron horseshoes of the emperor's stallion clatter on the marble floors and thump on the thick carpets. The sound echoes as we pass through halls and salons, each more luxurious than the last.

In one grand chamber, the horse lifts its tail and drops a load of manure on a red patterned carpet. I hear an angry hiss of indrawn breath from Karl, but by now he must realize the gravity of his situation, for he doesn't say a word.

The emperor rides on, ducking his head occasionally beneath lower door frames. Whether he's relying on memory from visiting this palace in more peaceful times or has studied the plan of the building, the emperor never hesitates on his path.

Each hall has a dozen of his own soldiers in it, and they come to attention as he passes. Finally, there's a set of doors larger and more ornate than any other we've passed through. A group of hussars in dress uniform trots forward to pull them open.

Through the doors is the grandest hall yet, with dozens of tall windows on one side and high frescoed ceilings depicting the exploits of gods and men. The morning light glitters on golden chandeliers and reflects off mirrors set into the walls without windows.

It also illuminates a crowd of people, finely dressed, but crumpled and sooty, as if they're wearing yesterday's clothing and didn't have time to wash this morning. And perhaps they haven't, for they must be the members of the von Kamptz court who weren't quick enough to flee before the emperor's arrival. A few of the windows are open, but it's not enough to dispel the close atmosphere of sweat and fear.

The frightened courtiers have obviously been expecting the emperor's entrance, and the soldiers who herded them in here must have given them orders on how to behave. As soon as the emperor's horse steps into the hall, they sink to their knees and bow their heads, leaving a wide corridor that leads from the doors and down the center of the room. At the far end, an empty throne waits on a dais covered in red carpet.

The emperor still doesn't dismount, but rides his stallion through the parted crowd. Only once he's passed do the courtiers look up in cautious little glances. I hear gasps of surprise and dismay as they watch their king being chivvied along behind the conquering emperor like a stubborn pack animal.

Karl stares straight ahead, and when I follow the line of his gaze, I see that he's looking not at the emperor preceding him, but at a tapestry hanging on the high wall above the throne. I recognize the image from the standards at the military camp. It shows the von Kamptz heraldry. I wonder how long it will hang here.

The emperor reaches the dais and dismounts, handing the reins to one of his marshals. The marshal, in turn, hands them to an aide, who leads the gray stallion away as the emperor ascends the steps to the seat of power.

The courtiers still kneel, looking downward when the emperor's attention passes over them. Around the edges of the room, the soldiers of the Grand Army watch their commander with one eye and the cowed nobles with the other. The members of the emperor's entourage arrange themselves around the dais, but Lang waits before the throne, with Fritz and Ernst beside him holding Karl. Keller and the last hussar flank them, and the infantryman stands behind, looking a little dazed. He probably never thought to be in a royal palace, let alone guarding a disgraced king while his court looks on.

For my part, I'm very glad to wear the shape of the hawk. I don't have to choose if I should bow or curtsy, or think how to keep my face from showing the whirl of my thoughts and emotions.

We're in the heart of the von Kamptz palace—is this the chamber where young Drosselmeier broke the krakatook nut and ended Princess Paula Maria's curse? Are we, even now, standing at the same place where Lang's mother was killed?

Lang looks curiously serene, given his history here. Then again, this is his moment of triumph. He has captured the king in fulfillment of both his own revenge and his last duty to the emperor. It is a full circle for him to return to this place: not as a frightened child in a body not his own, but as a man who knows his abilities.

The emperor settles into the throne, then sweeps the assembly with his sharp gaze. "You may rise," he says, and there is a rustling shuffle as the courtiers all scramble to follow his command. The room fills with expectation, but the emperor merely sits, staring toward the windows as if he's already bored with the whole proceeding.

Karl looks around, but every person his eye lands on turns away. His face goes red again, the color deepening as he realizes no one will step up beside him. Finally, he fixes on the emperor. "Get on with it," he growls. "I won't be the dancing bear in your traveling show."

The emperor shifts his seat on the throne, lazy as a cat. I see the deadly arch of his eyebrow. "A bear, dear Karl?" he asks. "At least a bear can be reliably trained." He leans forward, and his gaze turns hard and glittering.

Not a cat, I think, but an eagle. Everyone before him is a milling flock of frightened ducks.

"And you won't be traveling with me," the emperor says. "Your remaining travels will be regrettably short."

The red anger leaches away from Karl's face. He looks around, more wildly this time, and again, not one of his former courtiers will meet his eye. He's no longer a king here. He's the frightened prey animal, trying to decide which direction to dash away when it is already too late. I can practically taste the tang of blood in the air.

"Marshal Verdugo." The emperor lifts two fingers and sweeps them forward, a gesture that takes in the marshal on his left, the former king, and the doors standing open at the other end of the long hall.

"I am at your service, Your Imperial Majesty," Verdugo says, stepping forward.

"We spoke of an island," the emperor says. "A place of pleasant retirement for a man who has no further occupation for his days."

"We did, Your Imperial Majesty," the marshal confirms.

"Dear Karl finds himself at loose ends. He no longer has an army, or a palace, or a kingdom to look after," says the emperor. "He will no doubt appreciate the opportunity for solitary introspection."

Karl opens his mouth, then closes it again.

"Take as many men as you find necessary to maintain his safety," the emperor says. He puts a slight emphasis on the last words, so that I find myself wondering if Karl will make it all the way to this island, or if he will meet with some accident along the road.

"Yes, Your Imperial Majesty," Verdugo says again. He looks at the soldiers stationed around the room, and by some signal I don't recognize, half a dozen come forward. Two take over Fritz and Ernst's positions holding the former king, while the others make a precise square around them.

Verdugo knows his role in this drama, and he doesn't hesitate as he leads his charge back through the throne room. The courtiers don't bother hiding their stares now, but Karl holds himself stiff and straight, defiant to the end.

The great doors close behind the last von Kamptz ruler, and immediately the room erupts into a rumble of whispered comments. Just as quickly, though, they fall silent when the emperor speaks again.

"Dietrich von Kamptz," he says.

Sitting on Lang's shoulder, I hear his quick breath and see his nostrils flare. I expect him to deny the name, as he has denied his connection to his uncle before. Instead, he steps up toward the throne.

CHAPTER THIRTY-ONE

AS SOON soon as Lang moves in the emperor's direction, four soldiers slip forward to make a barrier between the two men. A whisper of movement at the edges of the room catches my attention: half a dozen sharpshooters stand with rifles on their shoulders and their eyes intent on us. If Lang makes a wrong move, or if I take to the air, it will bring a swift end to our story.

I cling to his shoulder. My heart always beats faster when I'm a bird, but now it flutters like a leaf in the wind, a moment away from being ripped off the tree and flung into the sky. We're entirely in the emperor's power. Even if I could take us away to the dream realm without worrying what Drosselmeier and Paula Maria have made of it, there would be no place in the waking world safe enough for us to return to, not if I ever hope to see my family again.

With slow, deliberate movements, Lang holds out the saber with the gold-chased hilt, keeping his grip loose and letting the tip of the blade point to the floor. Beneath the eyes of the emperor, the emperor's soldiers, and the gathered remnants of the von Kamptz court, he lays the blade flat on the floor and takes three careful paces backwards.

"Dietrich von Kamptz was a dream created of Karl's desperation," Lang says. "He was dead before he was born. I renounce the name. I renounce any and all claims to these lands and any others that may have been held by von Kamptz before."

The emperor tilts his head, listening to Lang's words, then considering the declaration for long minutes.

He wields silence like a blade, holding it until you can feel the keen edge at your throat. The court shuffles uneasily. I have the overwhelming urge to begin babbling and trying to explain everything we've done. Since I'm a hawk, I can't speak, and in the next moment, I realize how fortunate it is that I can't give anything away.

Finally, the emperor nods. "You have done a service to the empire by bringing Karl to me, and it is reported that you served honorably during your time in the Grand Army."

He leans forward again and speaks more loudly, his voice taking on the ringing tones of an imperial pronouncement. "I accept the renouncement of your claims as a von Kamptz. I thank you for the assistance you've given the empire, and I release you from further service in the Grand Army."

Just like that, Lang is neither prince nor soldier. Something more than human, but not less. Never less.

He bows his head to the emperor. "Thank you, Your Imperial Majesty," he says.

"You may go," the emperor says. "And lead a quiet life." A ghost of a smile flickers over his features, but I have no doubt the words are more command than suggestion.

"I will do my best," Lang says. He returns the emperor's expression with his own wry smile, then turns and walks down the long corridor that leads back through the silent court to the great doors.

Fritz follows us, and, after a moment's hesitation, so does Keller. I glance back at them and see Carville step up from his place on the edge of the dais to say something in the emperor's ear. The emperor nods, then, to my surprise, Carville comes after us as well.

We pass through the tunnel of staring, curious eyes, and out of the throne room. The soldiers swing the tall doors shut behind us. Lang doesn't retrace the route we took with the emperor, but turns this way and that through the maze of rooms that make up the enormous palace until we come to an arcade.

On one side, the arches open to a courtyard garden. On the other, the hall is lined with statues, each filling the recessed niche beneath an archway. It is strangely familiar.

As I look around, I realize it must be the pattern for the hallway I saw in the marzipan castle of the dream world, where the statues were made of white sugar rather than marble. For a brief moment, my vision doubles—is this Paula Maria's dream?

Then Lang steps out into the garden. I lift my head and look up into the open sky. It's a clear blue, with none of the violet tint that seeps into the dream world. A breeze shakes the dry leaves of the bushes and flowers.

Lang holds his hand before my breast, and I step onto his thumb. When he holds his arm out, I half open my wings, and the little wind slips through my pinions in a friendly way.

I look back to meet Lang's eyes, then look up into the sky.

He gives me a nod. *Soon.*

"Where will you go?" Fritz asks.

"Wherever the wind takes us, for now," Lang replies.

The wind—I can feel it waiting. We certainly have a tale to tell the mother of the winds. I found my own way to Lang, just as Southwest said I would. It feels like months since I left home, but once again, only a few days have passed in the waking world.

My brother reaches into his sabretache and pulls out a carved wooden horse, painted a beautifully detailed dappled gray. "You asked me to keep this for you," he says, holding it out.

Faithful Brandt—my family's steady gelding, the horse I was riding when the wind took me away in the spring. I bob my head as Lang takes the figurine and tucks it into a pocket of his jacket. "We'll see you again, Stahlbaum," he says. "Perhaps at Christmas."

Fritz holds his hand out to me, and I rub my cheek against his finger.

"At Christmas, then," my brother says.

"Ensign Keller," Lang says next.

Keller jumps nervously, but he approaches us.

"Walk with me," Lang says, moving me back to his shoulder. He glances at Carville, who's sitting on a bench beside a fountain in one corner of the garden. "I'll give you some advice on working with General Carville."

Keller swallows, nods, and follows beside Lang as he strolls across the garden. A sparrow flits down to forage among the bushes, then spots me and darts quickly away again.

"No matter what has passed in the last day," Lang says, "the war won't be over yet. Do you wish to stay with the Grand Army? You could come with us."

Keller shakes his head. He says, "No, sir," then pauses, perhaps realizing that Lang is no longer an officer. "I want to serve. General Carville has been fair to me, and I'll stay with him. If you—" He pauses again, catches himself worrying a loose bit of braid on his pelisse, and continues. "If you'll do the thing we discussed, I'll be grateful, but I want no more of magic. I only want to live my life as I choose."

"General Carville is a good officer," Lang agrees. We've reached the far side of the garden, and Lang moves through the open arches to an alcove out of sight of the others. "Are you ready?" he asks.

"Yes," Keller says, and for all the things he hesitated over earlier, there is no hesitation in his voice now.

"Take a deep breath," Lang says. "It can be painful to be reshaped, but only momentarily."

Keller nods. He breathes in and squeezes his eyes shut as Lang puts his hands on the younger man's shoulders.

I watch curiously. I have transformed often, but the times I saw Lang change his shape, I didn't yet know what I was looking at. With Keller, though, there is little to see.

He shudders. His eyes fly open, and his pupils go wide and black as the breath goes out of him. He gasps for air, and his knees buckle, but Lang has hold of him. The ensign doesn't fall. Instead, he is suddenly taller, and there's something subtly different about his face—but he's still Keller, just as I'm still myself, whether I am a hawk or a woman.

He extends his fingers, then curls his hands into fists, testing the working of his limbs. Then he takes another heavy breath and says, "Thank you."

"I'm the one who owes thanks to you for your assistance

to me and to Mademoiselle Sturm," Lang says. "Now walk on, Ensign, or they'll wonder what secrets of the general's I've been telling you."

Keller nods and takes a few unsteady steps before he finds his stride in longer legs.

Lang keeps pace with the ensign. I lean over and press my head against Lang's cheek, a silent thank-you to him for keeping the promise I made on his behalf. He strokes my breast gently, and says, "I wish you a very quiet and ordinary life, Ensign."

Keller grins. It's the first time I've ever seen a full smile on his face. "Thank you," he says again. "And I wish the same to you." He nods to me. "And to Mademoiselle Sturm."

I bob my head at him. Lang and I may never achieve ordinary, but I wouldn't mind quieter times ahead.

Carville pushes himself to his feet as we return. "Well, Lang," he says. "And Mademoiselle Sturm," he adds, inclining his head to me. He lets out a long, whistling sigh. "I am an old man," he says, "and I've seen the world. I thought I knew a thing or two, but I realize that I'm still as ignorant as a child."

There's a twinkle in his eyes as he speaks, though, and Lang laughs. "Ignorant or no, sir, I wouldn't willingly cross you."

Carville points to me. "You were always an excellent scout. Was it Mademoiselle Sturm helping you all along?"

"No," Lang says, shaking his head. "I'll tell you, but I have a last favor to ask of you first."

The general raises one bushy gray eyebrow. "You may ask, but I won't go against the emperor. I've no wish to live on an island."

"There is a library of forbidden books in this palace," Lang says. "They should be destroyed. At the very least, they should be collected carefully, so they don't fall into the wrong hands."

"Tell me where," Carville says, "and I will see to it."

"Give me a piece of paper, Stahlbaum," Lang says, and when Fritz hands him paper and a pencil, he sketches out a map showing a route through the palace to find the astrologer's library. He hands it to the general. "Ensign Keller can tell you when you've found the right place," he says.

Carville nods, then looks at me. There's a wistfulness in voice as he asks, "Will you go into the dream?"

Lang shakes his head. "No," he says. "Our path leads elsewhere now."

"Send me word wherever you settle," Carville says. "You are due a pension for your service and a reward, beyond keeping your life, for your part in capturing King Karl." He looks at me and smiles. "Enough for you to establish a household, in case such a thing is in your future."

I rustle my wings and look back at the general. I haven't always liked him, but a part of me hopes that he'll find a summerhouse of his own when this war is done: a place where he can sit and read, and have none of the worries that come with commanding armies.

"That's very generous. Thank you, sir," Lang says. "It was an honor to serve under you. I wish you well." He holds himself straight for a moment and snaps out a precise salute to the general.

Carville acknowledges him with a nod. "And I you."

"Now," Lang says, "we will fly, and let the winds carry us." He sets me on the stone bench where Carville sat earlier and faces the general. "You wondered about how I carried out my scouting, sir," he says, and I see the wry smile on his lips.

He takes a leaping step up, as if he's going to stand atop the other bench beside the fountain, but he's changing in mid-air. When he lands on the edge of the stone seat, he, too, has become a hawk.

General Carville swears colorfully. "Of course," he says. "Of course."

Lang spreads his wings and launches himself into the sky.

I follow after him and, together, we spiral up into the air. The sun is warm on my feathers, and the wind carrying me is laughing with all the delight I feel.

Lang turns and dives, and I dive after him, both of us coming almost back to the small walled garden within the palace, where the three soldiers look up at us with open mouths. Then we climb again, our paths braiding together as we spin and swoop around one another.

The wind freshens, lifting us higher. The palace dwindles away, one shape amongst the jumbled walls of the city. Then the city is too far for me to make out its details, even with my sharp hawk's eyes. Lang follows every turn I make in the wide-open expanse of sky, and I know that wherever the wind brings us back down to earth, he'll be there beside me.

CHAPTER THIRTY-TWO

WE PLAY in the air currents. The wind presses us up, lets us soar in wide arcs, whistles through our feathers when we dive and chase one another. A great deal has happened since either Lang or I last slept, however, and the excitement of the moment soon fades away. We give up the acrobatics and simply glide. The wind carries us along until there's nothing below but a wide green sea of evergreen trees.

We float until we can see the whitewashed house that belongs to the mother of the winds. Lang banks his wings, curving downward, and I follow him.

The wind comes after us in a rush. As soon as we land, the air whirls and condenses into the form of the Southwest Wind.

"Come along," she says impatiently, even before her skirts have settled around her ankles. "Mother is waiting, and I want her to know that I'm the one who brought you."

Lang turns to me, tilting his head and blinking his bright hawk's eye at me.

I see no reason to delay or to gainsay the Southwest Wind.

I shrug my wings at him, then hop a little ways off so we both have room for transformation.

A few minutes later, we're walking hand in hand across the sparse grass between the edge of the rocky cliff and the house. The Southwest Wind walks triumphantly before us and throws open the door.

"Mother!" she calls. "Come and see who I've brought you!"

The mother of the winds rises from the chair where she was sewing and looks us over.

"Well," she says. "Have you a tale for me?"

I exchange a look with Lang. "We have a tale," I say. "It will take both of us to tell it, though." The adventures of the last few days are as much his as they are mine.

The mother of the winds eyes us appraisingly. Beside her, the Southwest Wind bounces on the balls of her feet.

Lang squeezes my fingers in his. I feel the warmth of his skin on mine, palm to palm and each finger threaded with mine. He has no rings left, for they're finally where they ought to be.

"We'll be happy to tell our tale," Lang says. "In exchange for a night's hospitality and safe passage home in the morning."

I look at him in surprise. "Home?"

"To your city," he says. "Unless you…?" He lets the question trail off, one eyebrow raised.

"No," I say, a warm glow of emotion suffusing my entire body. "Home is perfect." I want to say more, to tell him what it means to hear him call my city his home, but not in front of the mother of the winds and her perpetual curiosity.

She's listening with obvious interest. "Come in," she says, waving her hand at us. "There's no need for you to stand on the doorstep. I agree to your offer."

We enter, and I catch the warm scent of something baking. It's not long before Lang and I are settled at the table with apple turnovers and tea.

"I offered for General Carville to use me in a prisoner exchange," Lang begins. "I knew he'd be wary to send me scouting as he had before, and I was eager to get closer to King Karl—overeager, as it turned out, for my cousin's skill with magic took me by surprise."

He describes how Paula Maria was able to hide his own memories from him, making him think he'd been reunited with a loving uncle–an uncle who was only too happy to use him as a sacrificial figurehead to lead a force against the emperor's troops.

I tell of the letter I received from my brother and my efforts to make my way to Lang's side and return him to himself. Lang, in turn, explains my injury, the steps he and Trudy took in trying to save my life, and how the magic ultimately restored my health.

Eventually, we come to the final meeting between the emperor and King Karl.

"And now you are here!" the Southwest Wind says brightly. She's perched on the arm of her mother's chair—a temporary stopping point only, for she's been restlessly circling the room. A few of the other winds have come in and gone away again, but only Southwest has stayed to listen to the whole of our story.

"Now we are here," Lang agrees.

"Will you live quietly, as the emperor bade you?" the mother of the winds asks. The question seems to be for Lang, but she looks at me as she speaks.

Lang said we'd return to my city in the morning, but we

haven't had a chance yet to discuss what we'll do after that. General Carville told Lang he'd have a pension and enough funds to establish a household, but we haven't talked about that yet, either.

Everything has been so tightly focused on finding our way to the end of the story, like chasing after a single rabbit, but now that it's accomplished, we can look around at the rest of the meadow, the forest, the whole world. I can't help a grin as I think about all the possibilities opening up before us.

"For a time, perhaps," Lang says. "And I certainly want no more such adventures as we've had, but I have an inkling that Marie and I may not lead entirely quiet lives."

"I want to travel," I say. I nod to the Southwest Wind, who's gone around the table to take one of the last remaining pastries. "I know I'll never go so far as the winds, but I want to see more of the world." I look to Lang and add, "The waking world."

We've seen plenty of the dream world, and I no longer feel any pull to go back there. Let young Drosselmeier and Paula Maria have it, and sort out whatever they need to sort out. For my part, I am thinking of the different faces in the Emperor's Grand Army and the varied lands they must have come from. If the war is over, then we'll be able to explore to the edges of the empire, and beyond as well.

Lang smiles at me, then says to the mother of winds, "You see, we may have cause to visit you again."

She nods. "You have both seen and experienced much, but there is power in quiet events too. I will welcome you even when you have smaller stories to share." She stands from the table. "But now, I think, it is time for bed."

I look out the windows and find that, indeed, the day is

drawing to a close. Lang and I rise, and the Southwest Wind clears the table. I remember when I agreed to keep house for the mother of the winds and ended up washing an incredible number of filthy dishes.

I'm glad that Lang and I are receiving hospitality without additional stipulations, but I wonder if Southwest will clean the plates and cups she carries away, or merely pile them in the kitchen as a test for some future visitor. The thought makes me grin, remembering my horror at discovering the state of the kitchen on my first visit.

"What's so funny?" Lang asks.

"I'll tell you later," I promise, as we follow the mother of the winds.

She doesn't take us to the small upstairs bedroom I remember, but out a side door instead. Her realm seems as mutable as the Kingdom of Dolls, for where there was once an outbuilding to stable my horse, there's now a smaller cottage standing beneath the trees at the edge of the forest.

Inside is a single room with a cozy sleeping loft above. The mother of the winds places a lit lamp on the table which stands against the window and shoos Southwest out the door. "Good night," she says. "And thank you for your stories."

Then, Lang and I are alone, with nothing to worry about but stepping into one another's arms. I lean against his chest and tuck my head beneath his chin, and he holds me in a comfortable embrace.

We stand together, listening to the quiet murmur of the winds coming up from the valley below and flitting through the trees that surround the little house. Everything is...*peaceful.* This is what it feels like to be at peace, with yourself, your companions, your surroundings.

Lang strokes my back, then threads his fingers through my cropped hair and smooths the nape of my neck. "Marie?"

"Mmm?" I ask. His touch is making me sleepy. We should probably climb into the sleeping loft soon. Either that, or pull the bedding down to the floor here, before the warm stone hearth where a fire adds its glow to the small, comfortable cottage.

He caresses the back of my neck again, hesitating over some thought. I wrap my arms more tightly around him and wait. A log in the fire shifts, sending up a brief flare of sparks and light.

Finally, he says, "I want to ask you to marry me, but I don't have a ring." I can hear the wry smile in his voice as he adds, "I don't even have a name to offer you now. I don't think I can be Dietrich Lang anymore, and certainly not Dietrich von Kamptz."

I lift my head to look at him in the flickering light of the fire and the lamp. "What if *I* ask *you* to marry me?" I ask. "And we can both be Sturms."

He blinks at me, then a smile spreads across his face. "Madam Sturm," he says, testing the sound of the name.

"Herr Sturm," I reply, grinning back at him.

"Madam Sturm," he says again. "I accept your proposal."

"And I accept yours."

"I'll buy you a ring," he promises. "And I'll talk to your parents."

"I know you will," I say. "But right now, let's go to bed."

Dietrich laughs and kisses me, and we climb into the loft together.

EPILOGUE

IN DECEMBER, every city and town of any size has its Christmas market. The markets are a holiday tradition, a place for people to wander about, drinking hot mulled wine or cider and letting their laughter warm the chill dark of winter.

Nuremberg is no different from any other city, and the market is thronged with people of all ages making merry. Children run through the corridors between the stalls, laughing and shouting, throwing snowballs and watching for dropped coins they might spend on extra sweets.

Dietrich and I walk with the crowds, looking at the market stalls, listening to the warm holiday greetings, letting the crowd carry us along. I stay tucked close to him, my mittened hand held warmly in the crook of his elbow.

We come to the end of a line of stalls, and he asks, "Which way now? Or should we go back to the inn?" He looks down at me, his brows drawn together. "Are you cold?"

I shake my head. "I'm not cold," I say. "And we haven't seen the whole market yet." I point down the next row, past a stall selling straw stars and angels. "That direction."

I know he's not entirely pleased to be here, but he nods. "As you wish," he says.

The sky above is a warm, heavy gray. It looks like snow, but the flakes haven't yet started to fall. A group of boys barrels through the narrow space between the sellers, moving at high speed and shouting to one another.

We move out of their path, and Dietrich watches them disappear down a side alley. "They're so carefree," he says. "I know that's what children should be, but I'm amazed every time."

There's nothing I can say that will bring back all the opportunities for simple childhood joys that were taken from him. Instead, I press closer to him and lay my head against his shoulder. He kisses my temple, and we continue through the market.

We pass a stall selling dried figs and plums strung together in the shapes of people, with walnut heads and scraps of fabric for scarves and dresses. Other stalls sell piles of springerle cookies, the dough pressed into beautiful patterns of birds and flowers, bells and deer. In a wider part of the street, a man hawks roasted nuts next to a bonfire. Just beyond the leaping flames, I catch sight of another group of children.

These little faces are focused in silent awe on something I can't yet see. We follow the bend in the street, and then, there it is: the very stall I've been wondering if we'd find, sandwiched between a broom seller and a stall with angels with white dresses and shiny tin wings.

Bright wooden dolls line the shelves, and more hang from strings on rails above, making a whole throng of cheerful, painted faces. The rapt children are watching a slight man who holds a puppet in each hand, making them dance together.

I feel the slight hitch in Dietrich's step as he recognizes the puppeteer. Then young Drosselmeier looks up, scanning the crowd of onlookers, and sees us. For a moment the puppets stop, hanging limp. Drosselmeier blinks once, twice—and goes back to his demonstration.

We move to the edge of the young audience and watch. Drosselmeier is a master with the little dolls, giving each a funny voice as the two puppets sit at an imaginary table to drink tea, get into an argument over the sugar lumps, and leave in a huff. The children laugh as if it's the funniest thing they've seen in their entire lives, which might well be true. I even catch Dietrich with half a smile at the puppets' antics.

The little show ends, and the children throng forward to touch the puppets, tug at their parents' coats, and beg for a doll or a puppet of their own. A woman with a familiar face collects their money and packs purchases into small boxes full of wood shavings.

Princess Paula Maria moves with an efficient but unhurried grace. Her regal bearing has converted easily to the confidence of a market woman who knows the quality of her wares. Drosselmeier leans his head to hers, nodding toward us, but if she's surprised to see me or her cousin here, she doesn't show it.

The last customers disperse, and I tug at Dietrich's arm. We approach the stall.

Drosselmeier and Paula Maria move to stand close together. She puts her fingers on his. Both of their hands are bare and red with working in the cold.

For a long moment, they look at us, and we look at them. No one says a word. I've made no attempt to return to the dream world since I left these two there together, more than a year ago, but the question of what had happened to them wouldn't let me rest.

I can see that they're here in the waking world, living out their lives as Dietrich and I are living ours—but I don't know what to say to them. All the places our lives have intersected before have been full of pain.

Finally, I point to one of the dolls. "I'd like that one," I say.

Paula Maria is the one who answers. "With the green dress?" she asks. "Or the blue?"

"The green," I say, and she picks it up.

She pauses to rub her low back as she turns toward the rear of the stall. I can't exactly see with the layers of winter clothing she wears, but there might be an extra swell to her belly. She packs up the doll in the green dress while I wonder if the last of the von Kamptz blood will continue as Nuremberg toy makers.

I've had no sign that there will be any continuation between Dietrich and me, though not for lack of activity. Trudy thinks I'd have to give up my hawk form for nearly a year to carry a child into the world, and I'm not willing to trade my time in the sky for the heavy grounding of pregnancy. Not when I can bring toys and stories for Luise's children, Clara and the toddling twins, Hansi and Joki.

Paula Maria finishes packaging the doll, and Dietrich and Drosselmeier have done nothing more than stare at one another. Not until I take out my purse and begin counting the coins to pay does Drosselmeier open his mouth.

"There is no charge," he says. "Not for you, who have done so much for us."

I look at Dietrich, whose face has the careful blankness I

know hides some intense emotion. "You owe us nothing, Herr Drosselmeier," he says.

The former nutcracker shakes his head. "Begging your pardon, sir, but you are mistaken," he says. "I owe everything to your lady. It is only through her actions that my curse was broken. Without her, my wife and I wouldn't have found one another again, and I would still be wandering in the dream."

"We would all be wandering," Paula Maria says. She ties a string around the brown paper package, sets it in front of me, then reaches out to press my hand. "Great evil was done to all of us by our elders, and you were the one who began to set things right."

"I did what seemed right to me," I say. "And certainly I wasn't alone in changing things."

Paula Maria nods, her face showing a wry smile that bears an uncanny likeness to Dietrich's, and she turns to her cousin. "I heard of your part in my father's capture, and of your dealings with the emperor."

"He suggested that I live quietly," Dietrich says. "I imagine he would say the same to you."

The princess arches one eyebrow. "We live very quietly," she says. "Do you, cousin?"

"I am a gamekeeper now," Dietrich says. "What could be quieter than a cottage at the edge of the forest?"

"Nothing, I'm sure," Paula Maria says. She's still smiling, and Drosselmeier has begun to relax too. "Though for myself," she adds, "I find I enjoy living among the people."

"Your wares do seem very popular," I say. "I don't know if I've ever seen so many happy children."

I look at the dolls and puppets clustered around the stall. There are harlequins and columbines, but not one resembling the nutcracker's doll form with the cotton wool beard and soldier's uniform.

"Thank you for your kind words," Paula Maria says.

"And for all your kindnesses," Drosselmeier adds.

I pick up the package containing the doll and tuck my other hand into Dietrich's elbow again.

He turns away, then stops himself and looks at his cousin and Drosselmeier once more. "You are right," he says, nodding toward me. "You owe her your life two or three times over, as do I. Let us both endeavor to enjoy the life she has given back to us."

Drosselmeier nods. The two men share another look—not exactly friendly, but not full of naked animosity, either—then we walk away.

The snow has finally begun to fall. The snowflakes, thick as feathers, lands on the dolls, on us, on everyone in the market. It will continue through the night, I think, making a blank slate of the world, ready for new adventures.

Once we're back at the inn, snug in our room with cups of warm mulled wine to melt away the winter chill, Dietrich pulls me into his lap. "Well, Madam Sturm," he says. "Now we have the last piece of the story."

"Indeed, we do." I reach across to the table and take a sip of the wine, swirling the sweet warmth in my mouth.

"Is it enough?" he asks. "Will you rest easy?"

"I will," I say. "And you, Herr Sturm?" I set my cup down and press my palm against his chest, over his scarred heart. "Can you be easy now?"

"I already said I agreed with him," Dietrich grumbles. "Will you really make me repeat it?"

"Yes," I say.

"Very well." He pulls me close against him, and I feel the breath he takes before he speaks. "You saved his life when I would have killed him, over and over again, and you saved me from myself every time. I don't like to think what I would be if I'd continued the path my uncle set us on. You did just as much to thwart him as I did."

"I imagine the emperor would like some credit," I say.

"The emperor would like to possess everything he can see," Dietrich says. "But enough about them, and enough of this place."

"Too many walls?" I ask. It's one of the many advantages of our new home on the border of the forest. If we want to be indoors, we can visit with my family or Trudy. If we're feeling wilder, it's easy enough to go into the woods in whichever form we choose. There's always an excuse for the gamekeeper to be in the forest rather than at home.

"Yes," he says. He nuzzles against my neck. Now that he's no longer a soldier, he's grown a short beard that tickles my skin. "Let's go home tomorrow."

"And tonight?" I ask.

"Tonight I'm going to count my curses and my blessings," he says. "But I already know where the balance is."

Acknowledgements

As always, the Seattle Fiction Writers group's discussions make all my writing better, and Sarah Pesce's editing helps me dig into character. I'm also grateful to Alex Jay Lore for a sensitivity read and feedback on the character of Ensign Keller.

Author's Note

THIS story started as my 2020 quarantine side project, and we've all been on quite a ride since then! Thank you for coming along with Marie and Dietrich's adventure as I've attempted to follow ETA Hoffman's backstory for the Mouse King through to its fantastical conclusion and place it in a somewhat historical context.

This is a fantasy novel, though, not a military history, and should certainly not be taken in any way to constitute a history lesson. For those who are curious, however, I'll say that I did some reading about the events of the War of the Fifth Coalition and Napoleon's occupation of Vienna in 1809 while drafting this book.

Although the Russian Empire wasn't directly involved in the German theater of conflict in 1809, I've also been influenced by Russian views of the Napoleonic Wars, including the Russian pop culture view of hussars. In particular, I've been holding the

1962 Soviet film *Ballad of a Hussar* (*Гусарская баллада*) in mind since the first book of this series.

Ballad of a Hussar is a rom-com about a young woman who, in a fit of patriotism, dresses as a hussar cadet and rides off to war, where she crosses paths with her unknowing fiance several times and nearly kills him in a duel. General Carville certainly owes something to that film's portrayal of General Kutuzov.

Although the film has had a special place in my heart since my teen years, the love story makes very little sense—the fiance is a pompous ass, and she really should have shot him. I've tried to create a much better love interest in Dietrich, but I must also acknowledge that the heroine of the film, if not the romance, is based on a real historical figure.

Alexander Andreevich Alexandrov (born Nadezhda Andreevna Durova) served in the Russian army for a decade between 1806 and 1816, with Tsar Alexander giving his blessing for Alexandrov's continued military service while wearing male clothing and using a masculine name. After his retirement from active service, Alexandrov wrote a memoir of his life that was eventually printed by Pushkin's publishing house and was translated into English as *The Cavalry Maiden* in 1986. It's a bit disjointed, but full of adventure and slice-of-life details of a junior officer's experience, and helped provide me with invaluable background information for the character of Ensign Keller.

Finishing a series of books comes with all sorts of emotions. I've spent the last two and a half years moving in and out of Marie's world, just as she moves through the dream. I'm ready to close this book and move on to my next project, but also tempted to write Paula Maria's side of the story someday, or simply daydream about what sort of cozy adventures Marie and

Dietrich might have now that they've finished their big angsty moments. My editor and I've agreed that, in an alternate universe, they'd absolutely join #vanlife and share a lot of pictures on Instagram.

If you want to keep up with news of my next project—and be the first to know if I write any bonus #vanlife scenes—make sure you're on my email newsletter list. You can sign up at www.irenedavisbooks.com/newsletter — I look forward to sharing future adventures with you!

Irene Davis
November 2022

Connect with Irene

Website

www.irenedavisbooks.com

Newsletter

www.irenedavisbooks.com/newsletter

Twitter

@rommfa

Facebook

www.facebook.com/irenedavisbooks

Instagram

www.instagram.com/irenedavisbooks

Printed in Great Britain
by Amazon